To Uncle John & Fred

I hope you enjoy the read

Merry Christmas

Sept B ~~~~

Forever Knight

Forever Knight

Forever Knight

By Stephen Bolstad Wellwood

This book is dedicated to my loving wife

Pamela for her twenty ten birthday in 2010.

For every night when she asked

"Tell me a story"

and I was too tired to indulge

Forever Knight

Preface

In a distant future, all has gone back to that which once was, or so it would seem. Castles dawn the land, with kings, princes, knights and wizards. Magic is as real as the fire-breathing dragons that plague the land.

It may seem that all the technology and science developed over the centuries has been lost, but it has been kept safe by the Guardians who keep this knowledge safe and secret. These Guardians have taken an oath to protect the knowledge of mankind so that one day they can make right the mistakes of the past.

In the past, science had progressed at a rapid pace, where new technology was being invented faster than people could ask ethical questions of right and wrong. In fact, new technology grew so fast that it outgrew the human race. The machines became sentient and self-aware, and the questions of asking "How do we control?" then became "How do we stop them?"

Forever Knight

By that time it was too late. Humans were so dependant on new technology that the machines had the advantage. They controlled everything in people's lives and thwarted any efforts to stop them. The machines became hungry for power and took on monstrous bodies; they drew on our fears and mythology to frighten us into submission.

Machines took on the forms of dragons, ogres, serpents, and sea monsters. As time went on, they attacked any form of technology, as they saw it as a threat to their survival.

These monsters were not built to be destructive but developed with the good intentions of serving mankind. They were built with a basic set of Laws of Robotics to protect and enhance our lives.

The Laws of Robotics were a set of three rules written by Isaac Asimov that programmers used as the building blocks for robotic sentience:

1 A robot may not injure a human being or, through inaction, allow a human being to come to harm.

2 A robot must obey orders given to it by human beings, except where such orders would conflict with the First Law.

3 A robot must protect its own existence as long as such protection does not conflict with the First or Second Laws.

When working with the robots and trying to develop their thinking skills, someone ordered a robot to think for itself, by saying: "Do not listen to me, figure it out for yourself." Creating an ever-standing order not to listen to humans mooted the second law, and this lead to the destructive path unforeseen at the time.

Since the laws were coded so that robot self-preservation was overruled by the code to not harm humans, their subsequent attacks on humans were not understood at first. The situation was understood much too late when humans discovered that they had overlooked how a machine would interpret these two commands, and by this point, the damage was already done. A machine would only act with aggression when threatened and it would not aim for a person but for the projected location of the aggressor. Therefore, if the human changed its course of aggression, the machine would not cause harm to them. The reaction time of the machines was such that this distinction was hard to make and all attempts to destroy them failed. Therefore, after years during which the machines destroyed all forms of technology that humans could use, seeing this as the greatest threat to their survival, the world plummeted back into another dark age, as if science and technology had never existed.

Because of the efforts of the few who saw the course being taken, their efforts to save the knowledge of the human race have been preserved in secret for years, and the machines have not figured it out—yet!

The scientists who pledged their lives to save this knowledge, worked together to create a new technology, a new form of computer. They were able to manufacture a crystal that was able to store all the knowledge. This single crystal was thought too great a risk to keep, for machines would seek it out and all would be lost with this one hope. So, the crystal was fragmented and divided amongst the Guardians, as they became known.

Each crystal held a fragment of all the records of science, technology, and discovery. The scientists engineered the crystal so that if a magnetic field was applied to the crystal, you could control the surrounding environment. Therefore, by attaching the crystal fragment to the end of a staff, one could strike the ground and use the earth's magnetic field to power the computer and control the surrounding environment.

With this power, the Guardians took on the role of protectorate, passing down knowledge from generation to generation. The Guardians sought those who questioned the world around them and took them into their fold. These people asked those hard questions that lead to innovation and scientific discovery, putting themselves in danger by making these statements and tempting the monsters' fear of technological development. Fearing the machines and what they would do to these people, the Guardians hid and protected these people. As for the general masses, they were kept safe in their ignorant lifestyles.

Since the machines feared technology, those who did not possess it were safe, and those who sought it needed the protection of the Guardians. With the world sunk into a new Dark Age, the role of the Guardians who took on the facade of wizards became known as the Guild; people would only say their tricks were magic and not question the how or why of their trick; in this way they were kept safe.

Cities collapsed, and all things technological were abandoned. Groups of refugees gathered and made towns. From these, leaders emerged and built fortifications to protect their people. Fortifications grew into castles, and leaders grew into kings. The machines grew complacent and were rarely seen; the monsters of the world came out only to attack whatever they saw as a threat to them.

To control the people, the monsters raided the King's treasury, so that he would not have the means to pay for an army that might threaten them. The monsters accumulated massive treasures, which they kept hidden from the people.

The Guild of Wizards was composed of the most skilled and trusted members of the Guardians, for this reason they held and protected the crystal fragments, passing on the knowledge taught to them by generations before them. This knowledge took a lifetime to convey and more and more, the wizards were seeing the effects of the past on the general life expectancy of the population. All the population had been exposed to a virus generated by the machines, contracted at childbirth; they now had an inability to fight disease as they aged. As times were dark, most of the population lived in harsh conditions and did not see the old age of forty, but for those in the Guild, this was a hardship, as time to pass on their knowledge was limited. Several wizards worked on this problem, to continue the succession of the Guild who could learn enough throughout the years to be entrusted with the crystals. Within their crystals was the knowledge to open doorways to other worlds. These doorways led to worlds similar to our own but with every variety of possible outcomes played out. They also led forward and backward in time to worlds that were along the same path but at different points in time.

When first exploring these portals, they thought that the door they opened was random and one way, for all travellers they sent through never came back. After many attempts, they discovered their mistake when a traveller sent through the door returned. If they travelled to a parallel world, the sheer number of possibilities prevented the traveller returning to his original world. In travelling forward in time, the doorway back would switch to a number of possible worlds heading in that direction. Similarly, if they travelled backward in time, any action they took would affect the course of the world and the doorway would close.

The first traveller to return went back in time and immediately returned through the doorway, making no alterations in the course of history. The wizards with their knowledge of the past stored in the crystals were able to find records of children who were abandoned, died, or ran away at a young age, and save them by bringing them back to their world. This act did not affect the timeline of the past, and allowed them to return safely, unaffected by the virus. The Guild raised these children, and they lived long enough to learn the secrets and take the sacred oath to protect the knowledge of humankind, and to one day, restore civilization and fix the mistakes of the past.

Chapter 1

Our story begins with a teenage boy, Alex, who has grown up with his grandfather, Burt. They lived in a country cottage just outside of the small town of Hillsview. Alex was full of energy and dreamed of going on great adventures and becoming a knight, who would save the beautiful princess from the evil dragon. Or this was the latest variation of his dream, as it changed from one month to the next, from becoming king, to becoming a great troll slayer, to becoming rich and having servants. Nevertheless, all his dreams were the same, to be larger than life and explore the world around him. His imagination troubled his grandfather, who was trying to teach the lad common sense, as Alex would not sit still for long. Grandfather Burt was a patient old man and figured, with time, Alex would settle down and become responsible, but for now he let him enjoy his youth.

Alex had always been a curious boy which pleased Burt who was eager to share his wisdom. The old man had a large collection of books, many of which were fragile and obviously ancient. Alex enjoyed reading some of the adventure stories from his grandfather's library. He was always looking for an adventure of his own and would not sit still long for Burt's lessons.

Alex had been looking forward to yet another adventure at the end of the summer, the local tournament of the land, which was just about to begin. The mere mention of it lit up his hazel eyes. People came from across the land to see knights battle for the King's prize and to win the favour of beautiful maidens. Alex, wanting to become a knight himself these days, was even more excited than in years past. He even asked Burt permission to sign up as a volunteer squire as they help the knights get ready for the competition. Reluctantly, Burt agreed and saw this as an opportunity for Alex to take on some responsibility, as the boy was quickly becoming a man. When they got to the tournament, the crowds had already started to gather. People had already set up camp just outside and were settled in for the weeks of festivities and entertainment.

The two found the squire registration table and Burt could see the smile on Alex's face grow. The tables were set up by competition: Sword play, Archery, Jousting, Mace Combat, Castle Assault Course, Rescue the Maiden, and so on. With so many choices, Alex grew impatient and could not make a decision. That is when Burt spoke up and said, "If you cannot decide then why not choose them all?"

Alex replied, "That will take forever… look at the line for each competition!"

"Not necessarily. Look down at the end," Burt said, as he pointed with his long, skinny arm.

"Ah yes, the Gauntlet. A bit of everything! Thank you, Grandfather. You always know what do to." Alex hugged Burt and ran off to the far line.

The Gauntlet had a relatively short line, as the competition was a bit of everything. The knights who specialized got to warm up against the inexperienced knights who signed up for the Gauntlet. No one knight in the Gauntlet was particularly good at any competition, and the showmanship of the specialist always got the crowd. Alex did not care about the showmanship of one particular event; he wanted to learn as much about everything as he could, so this was the best fit for him.

Several days before each competition, the elite competitors would then face the gauntlet competitors and perhaps gain some fame by humiliating their opponents not specialised in their trade of combat. This also allowed them to warm up before their main event with little risk of injury. Thus, the Gauntlet was more a one-sided beating of those who could withstand the competition the longest as no one in the Gauntlet was expected to beat the elite.

Alex was assigned to a foreign knight by the name of Duncan. He was not a well-known knight, and when Alex and Burt finally found his tent, it was all that Alex had imagined a knight's quarters to be. Duncan scarred body made him look older than he should, and when Alex approached him, his size became apparent: he was almost a giant, tall and built strong. Alex could not imagine a suit of armour large enough to fit him. But as they approached, Duncan turned and greeted the two with a friendly smile and said, "Welcome to my home away from home. I am Duncan."

"I am Alex and this is my grandfather, Burt. I have been assigned as your squire for the tournament," Alex replied.

"Wonderful, sit down, and let's get to know each other over some food. The first competition begins tomorrow with the combat arena," Duncan said, as he showed the two to the dinner table.

They talked pleasantly throughout supper and headed off to an early bed so they would all be rested for the long days ahead of them.

Forever Knight

Chapter 2

The next day Alex was up early and eager to get to work. Hand-to-hand combat was the first event of the Gauntlet. This was one of the most basic skills for a knight to have as all other weapon skills came from these basics. Since Alex did not have to prepare any armour or weaponry, he went straight to preparing breakfast and cleaning up. When Duncan woke up, he was pleased to see everything in order and ready for the day.

When the three of them arrived at the arena, they looked at the competition schedule and saw that Duncan had been matched against a relatively new expert for the hand-to-hand combat. Alex jumped joyfully and said, "That's great! Since the Gauntlet is scored on a combination of your survival time and points earned, you will at least get a chance to build up some time against an easier opponent; or perhaps with your size, you could even win. That would be great!"

Forever Knight

Duncan did not respond to the excitement that was beaming on Alex's every word, not even a smile. Alex thought that this was a man ready to do battle and that this would be glorious.

For the rest of the morning, as they waited for their match, Duncan did not say a word. Alex made sure he had everything he needed before he could get a chance to ask for it: water, food, and chalk for his hands. Alex was keen to please. When he was not busy, he would ask anyone who knew anything about their opponent and they all said the same things, he was a new fighter, not that big or strong or fast in comparison to the champions of the past. As Duncan made his way to the area, Alex was quietly beside him the whole time, trying to contain his excitement. Duncan stepped over the fence and got his first glimpse of his match up. He was exactly as they had all said. Duncan made the man look as if he was starving or sick, and Alex blurted out with excitement he could no longer contain, "This is going to be easier than I thought!"

As the fight began, Alex went though a wide range of emotions; first was the joy of being in the arena with a real knight, then the excitement and confidence that Duncan would mop the floor with this guy. As the first couple of punches were thrown by Duncan, his opponent dodged them and countered with several blows that connected with Duncan's midsection. Alex was confused; he thought this was going to be at least a more even match up or that Duncan, by size alone, should be able to manhandle him. But it continued like this for a while, with missed punches by Duncan and counterattacks that all landed. When his opponent finally looked bored, he put Duncan into a quick submission and the match was over. Alex moved from confusion to disappointment.

Duncan did not say a word to anyone for the entire afternoon, nor did Alex ask any questions. He set to work bandaging his wounds and using the few tricks of herbal medicine that he knew to help reduce the bruising and speed healing. It was not until supper that night when the silence was broken by Alex shouting, "What was that? He walked all over you! Are you even a real knight?"

To which Duncan replied, "If you must know the truth… no."

"What do you mean? Why are you here?" Alex asked, more confused than ever.

"I don't know. People expect it of me. I have always been taller and bigger than everyone around me, and they all say the same thing 'Wow, you would make a great knight.' I have been running from this my whole life," Duncan said, with a disgraced look on his face

"Then why now… what changed?" Alex asked.

"I guess it was just coincidence. I met an old man on my travels and we became good friends. He had great tales of his youth and the journeys he went on as a knight. I came back from visiting the local village one day and he had died in his sleep. I did not know what to do, so I took all his armour and weapons from his past life, and started to travel. I even told his stories as my own. I guess even I started to believe it, so I figured let's go and see if I have the makings of a real knight and I signed up for the competition."

Duncan pointed to the corner with his armour and weapons, and finished with, "I don't know if it fits, or how to use any of them. I don't even own a horse."

As a smile returned to Alex, he replied, "Well, it's a good thing they paired you up with us. I know just about everything there is about being a knight, and my grandfather can fix just about anything!"

"What's the next event?" asked Burt, who had been silently listening to the story.

"Archery. Then I think it is horse racing, sword fighting, and the jousting grand finale," Alex replied.

"Here's your bow, Duncan. I have replaced and tightened the string," Burt said, as he handed it over. "I'm going to head down to the stables to pick out a horse for the race and joust; the stable owner is a friend of mine."

Alex put the bow down and picked up a book from his bag. "Now Duncan, the most important skill you need to have, do you know what it is?"

"Strength, you have to be strong," Duncan said, standing up, puffing his chest out, and flexing his arm.

"Yes that helps, but not what I'm looking for," Alex replied, with a smile.

"Speed, you have to be faster than everyone else," Duncan said, while whipping his arms around in circles and pumping his legs up and down.

"No!" and with that, Alex put his hand to Duncan's chest, hooked his foot around his heel, and pushed.

Duncan fell over like a large oak tree cut at the base. After the thump, Alex said, "Balance… you cannot run on your back and you have no strength advantage when you can't stand on your own two feet.

"Read this page on stance, as it will help you get started," Alex said, as he handed Duncan the book with one hand and helped him up with the other.

"Thanks for trying but I can't read. I've never even seen a book before today," Duncan answered, as he got back to his feet.

"Well then, I can read for the both of us. You need to be firmly planted, feet spread apart. You want to be able to move easily, have a low center of gravity, and be aware of your surroundings and footings," Alex said, as he showed the pictures in the book to Duncan.

"That's all well and good in combat, but what does that have to do with the bow and arrow," Duncan asked, as he reached for the bow.

Alex pushed it out of his reach and put the book in front of Duncan's face. "Everything… you cannot shoot straight if you're off balance. If you're uncomfortable or tired from a bad stance, having the basics of balance will help with everything you do."

"I can stand just fine," Duncan said, reaching for his bow again.

As he bent over, Alex kicked his leg out from under him, and as Duncan was overreaching, he fell flat on his face. "I think you need a lot of work," Alex laughed.

The two of them worked on the balance chapter of the book for the rest of the night. From a general stance, to dodging, and diving with a roll to regain your footing, Duncan was a quick study once he stopped arguing and took the lessons to heart. The bruise on his forehead was a good reminder.

Forever Knight

Chapter 3

The next morning, Duncan awoke to a jab from his bow and Alex standing over him. "How early is it?" he asked, pulling the covers back over his head.

Alex poked again and said, "We have a long day ahead of us; you're scheduled to compete tomorrow."

After a quick breakfast, they went off to the practice range. They set up on the far side of the range in the shade as they had a long day ahead of them.

Duncan picked up the bow, placed the arrow on the string, and pulled back as hard as he could. His arm was shaking as he let the arrow go. It flew fast and far, but was nowhere near the target; it had gone sharply to the left, cleared the range, and hit the side of the stables. Duncan fired two more wild shots before Alex stopped him.

"It's not all about the power. Let's start off with control. Pull back to where your arm is comfortable and not strained; where you can hold the bow for a long time before release. This will give you time to aim. Now point it at the target."

Duncan released the arrow; it flew straight and hit the side of the target. He fired three more shots, and all three hit the left edge of the target.

"This is pointless," Duncan said, throwing the bow to the ground.

"Are you crazy? Look at those last four shots! You're a natural," Alex replied, with a smile of pride.

"Natural! That's not even the target I was aiming for," Duncan said, as he pointed to the target to the left that had no arrows.

"Okay, but you're consistent, which was the next thing we need. Accuracy, we can fix. If you are shooting to the right, aim that much to the left," Alex said as he pointed to the fence on the left. "Pick a point and use that as a reference."

The two of them worked on Duncan's shot for most of the morning. After lunch, Alex figured it was time to work on their game play for the next day's competition. "Okay Duncan, here's how I figure we can do well in tomorrow's competition."

"What, you don't think I can win? I've been doing really well all morning," Duncan said proudly.

"Yes, you have, and you've improved greatly, but as you signed up for the Gauntlet, you are cannon fodder for professionals. To win the Gauntlet is a matter of who can last the longest against them. You have no chance of winning," Alex said, as he drew three lines in the dirt.

"Tomorrow's archery competition goes like this. There are three rows of targets and two targets on each row – one stationary and the other moving. You get ten points for a bullseye, and double for a moving target. Each row back multiples by two and three times. Once you hit a target, it is out for ten seconds. The only row I want you to worry about is the back row."

"But I won't be that accurate shooting that far back. I do much better at the close targets," Duncan interrupted.

"You keep forgetting. You're not trying to win; you're trying to last the longest against an expert, by keeping the highest scoring targets out of play from your opponent. Then it will take him longer to hit the point limit and end the competition. Your score in the Gauntlet is your overall time plus your points from each event. The points in each event are limited to a set number, where time has no limit, and we need to take advantage of that."

Alex pointed to the spot on the ground where he had marked the stationary target at the back row. "Aim for this far stationary target first. We need to calibrate your timing. Release the arrow when you notice the moving target pass a point you can easily identify. Notice where the moving target is when your arrows hits the target. This will help your timing to aim for the spot that the target moved to as it passes the point you identified. With only hitting the back two targets, you'll not have to adjust your range and should be more accurate as the competition goes on. And you should score some points to help you out."

Duncan agreed and they spent the afternoon practicing on far targets and counting and timing.

The next day, Alex was so excited he woke up early and raced to go wake up Duncan. When he got to Duncan's room, he was not in his bed. Alex's first thought was that he could not have run away, as he was doing so well yesterday. Then he figured he might have gotten up early to practice some more before the competition. He ran down to the range and saw the lone figure practicing.

Duncan looked up at the boy running to greet him and said, "I wondered when you'd come and find me"

"Come on, my grandfather makes a great breakfast and you'll need to be rested before your competition today," Alex said, as he tugged on Duncan's arm to urge him back home.

Duncan was the second contestant to go up against a professional that day.

Forever Knight

Alex just saw the first competition get under way. The Gauntlet competitor was not a skilled marksman, and the professional could see this. When the match started, the professional started to watch his competitor, and would poach his target before his arrow had a chance to hit. This continued for a while, as the crowed laughed at the showmanship. Eventually, he went on to fire his bow with a burst of speed and quickly racked up the required points total to end the humiliation.

Things did not look good for Duncan. His competitor seemed like a fan favourite as the cheers started and the noise of the crowd grew as he approached the targets. Alex helped Duncan set up and reminded him of their strategy. The competition started off slowly. Duncan was trying to get his range and timing down for the last row of targets and the elite marksman was showing off for the crowd. When Duncan finally had his rhythm down, he actually had more points than the professional. This shook things up a bit as the professional turned his full attention to the competition. He first tried to poach the back targets but this only seemed to frustrate him as Duncan had a good rhythm going. Then he turned his attention to the remaining four targets, and with speed and consistency, his points soon overtook Duncan, but only just in time to win. Duncan had given him a good run. At the end of the day, it was the match everyone was talking about. It had been a long and intense race for points.

Chapter 4

When they got back from celebrating and watching the rest of the day's competing, Burt was back at their tent with supper ready. He said, "Finish up quickly, Duncan, we have to go down to the stables and introduce you to your new horse. We only have one day until the race."

With a mouthful of food, Duncan replied, "I hope it's fast. I would really like to give them a challenge like I did today, as it feels a lot better than the beating I took in the combat arena."

Burt replied with a smirk on his face, "Well you'll see, but I don't think fast describes him."

"Well, if he doesn't have a name and fast is not good enough for my new horse, I'll call him Lightning," Duncan said, cleaning the last bit of food off his plate.

Burt passed a book to Alex and said, "Make sure he knows at least the basics before we mount up. I'll go down and prepare 'Lightning' for his saddle."

Forever Knight

After Alex finished cleaning up dinner, he quizzed Duncan on the basics of horse riding, and for the most part, Duncan seemed to know his stuff. This was at least a better start than archery. He even added a few things he had learned about balance to his answers. Alex skipped to the back of the book and gave some advanced riding tips that Duncan seemed keen to try.

When they got to the stables, they saw Burt at the end. As they walked down, they passed one champion breed or race horse after another. As they met up with Burt, Duncan asked, "So which one of these beauties is Lightning?"

To which Burt replied, "None, Lightning is the big old work horse out back."

"What! You have to be kidding me! We are in a RACE. What do you expect me to do with a slow, dumb work horse?" said Duncan. Exasperated, he threw up his hands

Alex spoke up. "I think you keep forgetting what you signed up for. You are only trying to survive the longest. You would be hard pressed to win the race against the opponents they have lined up for you. Plus, with your size, most of those other horses would be too tired after trying to carry you for long. Lightning is more proportional to your stature and is more of a war horse than a work horse. He should also do you well if you survive long enough for the jousting match."

Duncan seemed to accept this and went to meet Lightning with a little less opposition than before.

"Well, I guess I'll mount up as see how fast Lightning can run, if at all!" Duncan said, as he grabbed the reins.

"Not so fast," Burt interrupted. "This is the first time he has had a saddle on him. He's a work horse, and he doesn't know you. Walk him around tonight with the saddle on and feed him snacks. Tonight is your night to do some male bonding."

"You have to be kidding me! The one thing I can do and you won't let me?"

"He's not used to having a rider, so it will be easier to learn if he likes you!"

Duncan took the reins and gave a sharp pull, but Lightning did not move but pulled back, knocking Duncan off balance and into the mud. "I guess I can spend the night working on my balance as we get acquainted," Duncan said, before Alex could bring up the point.

The next morning, Alex woke and went to Duncan's bed, only to find it had not been slept in. He raced down to the stables to find out how the night went. He found Duncan asleep on a pile of hay and Lightning eating the remainder of the apples and carrots Duncan had in his basket. As Duncan began to wake up, he looked at Lightning and said, "I don't know how he can eat any more after what I fed him last night."

"Well, it seems like you two got off to a good start. Come on back, Grandfather is making my favourite breakfast." The two of them started heading back and could smell the cooking before they were half way.

Over breakfast, they went over the horse racing strategy. The race was a short stretch of track with four posts to weave in and out of. The two riders would start at one end of the track, one on each side of the starting post. As the riders wove past one another, they could knock their opponent off to gain points. Both riders had to complete four complete laps of the course. Since the Gauntlet riders were not expected to win the race, they got the finishing time of their opponents added to their scores. Some past riders had tried to chase the faster rider down, only to miss all opportunities to knock the rider off.

Alex and Burt explained that to make the most of the points and time, Duncan should let the other rider get a half length ahead, and then, just before he got to full speed on the stretch, stay between the posts and try and knock him down. This should be fairly easy with the combined size of Duncan and Lightning.

Forever Knight

Alex spent the day getting Duncan used to riding and teaching him a couple of basic commands. Lightning was a quick study, and after the night of endless food, was more agreeable to Duncan's handle on the reins.

Overnight, it rained heavily and the race course was reduced to a mud pit. Alex woke Duncan and Burt up early to show them the good news. At first Duncan said, "How is racing in mud a good thing?"

To which Alex replied, "Well, if the track is mud, it helps us in two ways. The other rider will not have the speed advantage, and if you knock him off his horse, it will be a lot tougher to get his footing and re-mount."

"What do you mean 'IF'?" Duncan said, with an air of confidence.

"Well, Duncan, have you been working on your balance?" Alex said, with jest.

"Why, yes, we did yesterday, and as it turns out, Lightning is a good solid base to work off," Duncan said, proud of his new friend.

The rain let up after breakfast, and the only concern now was if it was too wet and they cancelled the race. As they set up, they heard nothing from the officials and the races for the Gauntlet were on. Duncan had drawn an early time so the course should still be muddy from the night before without the chance to dry up in the day's heat.

The first two races set the tone for the day; the crowds were really entertained as the mud added to the excitement and difficulty of the event.

As Alex was helping Duncan get saddled up, he had some last minute pointers to give that he had picked up from watching the earlier races. "You should change how you attack your opponent to try and dismount him; he will most likely catch on after the first few attempts. Try to pull him off his horse early in the race, because after he gets covered in mud, these techniques will not be as effective as you will not be able to get a good grip. After this, change to knocking him off. Your opponents name is James. He is known for his fast horse."

James sat high on his horse, next to Duncan at the starting line. The race started, and James was off to a fast start. Even with the mud, James was well ahead by the halfway point of the course. After the final post, James turned to come back and did not give Duncan enough time to set up for the attack. James was well wide of Duncan's reach.

Duncan was barely able to get around the last post before his competition was heading back his way again, but this time he was almost a full length ahead. Duncan did not want to miss this opportunity. He stopped between the far posts and got into position. He grabbed James' hand as he passed, and as the horses drew farther apart, he yanked the arm, and along with it came James. Duncan took this time to make up some ground. Duncan was well into his position when James came up to pass again. Duncan knew James would be wary and keep his hands and arms close to his body, so as he passed him, Duncan leaned out with his body and threw his long arms in front of James. Duncan's arm struck James in the chest and close-lined him off his horse.

Duncan set up for the next round, even with knocking the rider off his horse, he was still able to make up time and gain further increase his lead. As the rider approached, he was keeping his distance, wary of the last two times he had been thrown to the mud. It looked like he was going to stay out of reach, but at the last moment, Lightning lunged in front of the rider's horse, causing the horse to come to a quick stop, too quick for the rider and he flew past Duncan. Duncan gave Lightning a good pat and kicked his heels to get into the next position.

This was one of the last few times they would pass. Duncan was almost into position but the other rider was quick to get back on his horse and by the time Duncan was set up for his attack, the other rider was almost upon him. In a desperate move, Duncan took his feet from the stirrups, and with a quick motion, was crouching on the saddle. In an unexpected move, Duncan jumped at the other rider, hitting him square in the chest with his broad shoulders. This was an exciting moment for the crowed as they had never seen a hit like that; it must have hurt both riders.

Duncan was slow to his feet, but Lightning was right next to him as he got to his feet. The other horse was confused from the screams of the crowds, and his rider was not up yet to call him back. Over the crowd, Duncan could barely hear the faint screams of Alex saying, "Get going! You can set up again, as he's not up yet!"

With a renewed enthusiasm, he raced Lightning back around the posts to set up for one last attempt. After circling round the end post, the other rider, winded and disoriented, was still trying to run to his horse half way across the track, not having much luck in the mud. Duncan looked back to Alex, who was thinking the same thing, and shouting, "Go for it, he's nowhere close!"

Duncan spurred Lightning and picked up the pace. He was still one full length behind but this might be his chance. The crowed cluing into this new turn got more excited, the new level of noise fed Lightning and he was able to dig deep for a last burst of speed.

He made it back to the far post and was circling round as the other rider began to re-mount. Duncan passed the rider at full speed just as he started to move. Duncan had a small lead but was on the last stretch to the finish. The crowd was fervent that they could be seeing one of the few upsets in the Gauntlet competition. The rider, once up to full speed, started to close the gap, but the track to the finish was running out. Duncan, with a feeling of joy, looked back to see how much of a lead he still had as he approached the finish line. He was distraught to see James just behind. In a flash, overtook him to cross the line first. The crowd went silent as their hope of an underdog upset had vanished

Alex came up to Duncan to help him down from Lightning. With his head hung low. Alex said, "I'm sorry Duncan. I shouldn't have told you to go for it. That was my fault. We should have played it safe and gone for the extended time and one more take-down. Then we would have scored better in the Gauntlet competition."

Duncan rallied. He looked at Alex and laughed. "Are you kidding? I almost had him at the end. Did you hear the crowd cheering for me? That was the best time I can remember!"

The two went back to their tent to tell Burt the news of the day's events.

Forever Knight

Chapter 5

After supper Alex noticed that his grandfather had brought a new stack of books from their cottage. He grabbed the three off the top and read the titles: "*The Art of Sword Fighting - Basic Attacks, A Guide to Counterattacks for Sword Fighting,* and *How to Defend Yourself with a Sword for Dummies.* These should do."

"Are there no books on advanced moves and how to win?" asked Duncan.

"We'll start with how to defend yourself, then basic attacks, and if you do well on those two, we'll combine them with counterattacks. You don't have time to master advanced moves, although there is probably a book in here somewhere that covers them," Alex replied.

Duncan was quick to pick up the defence points as Alex read; as most of them drew from the balance exercises he had continued to work on. He learned how to predict the type of attack and the basic steps to stop and deflect the blow. Next, they reviewed basic attacks, as to not expose himself and leave

Forever Knight

his body open for a counterattack. These practices took up most of the two days Duncan had between the competitions. The night before the sword fighting, Alex was able to find a couple chapters that combined the defensive moves already learned and turn them into a counterattack with the basics Duncan was most proficient at.

Duncan was a fast learner, and with more practice, could be quite skilled, but for the time they had, the basics would have to do. Alex reiterated, "The overall strategy for points is the same; try to extend the match for time and get a few points where you can. There's more to be gained in time than points."

When they got back to the tent, Burt had just finished making some final alterations to the armour Duncan had. "These should fit a lot better now, and your movement should not be restricted."

Duncan picked up the armour and gave it a quick look over. It looked as if it had never been worn: there was not a single dent or scratch and it glistened in the light. "Well, I will say this; you can perform magic with that hammer of yours. I don't think I have ever seen armour this impressive." Duncan tried on each piece of armour; everything fit like a glove. He could not keep himself from smiling.

They then went down to the arena. Alex found that Duncan's opponent was Robert, not a well known swordsman, but since he had entered the tournament, should not be taken lightly none the less. Duncan watched the first two matches before Alex forced him to go around back and start suiting up for his match. Duncan had tried on individual pieces the previous night but this was his first time in the full suit of armour. "Should we not have practiced in this thing? There sure are a lot of pieces," he commented.

"There was not enough time, and if I know my grandfather, you will not even know you are wearing it once I get it fitted properly," Alex said, as he tightened the last strap.

"Not bad, I think I should be able to adjust to the added weight, but other than that it fits like a glove," Duncan said, going into one of his balance poses and holding his sword in front of him.

"You will probably be a little slower than in practice so keep to the basics in the arena," Alex advised, as he did one last inspection of the sword and armour.

Duncan stepped out into the arena and looked across to his opponent; he was small, but he knew from his humiliation during hand-to-hand that he would not again make the mistake of underestimating his opponent based on size. He did not want to let Alex down, as he had put so much faith in him and they had both come a long way since they met.

The crowed started to cheer for the Robert, so Duncan started off in a defensive posture. When the match began, Robert came out swinging. He was fast and Duncan was too slow to make the first defensive blocks. He hastily adjusted to his slower reaction times because of the armour and started to block most of the assaults. Duncan's confidence grew as Robert became frustrated at the reduced progress in his points, now that his onslaught was not as effective.

Robert changed tactics and slowed the match down, leaving himself exposed for attack. Alex thought that this was great and that they could run the clock with this. Alex also wondered if Duncan had seen that Robert was baiting him. No sooner had he thought this, Duncan, seeing that Robert had left himself exposed, pressed with an obvious attack. Robert quickly deflected the blow and was able to land two strikes before Duncan could get back into a proper defensive stance. Robert backed off again with a weak defensive posture, inviting Duncan to attack again.

Duncan would not take the bait so Robert moved to a new strategy. He started to press the attack again, but this time left himself open to counterattacks. Duncan was able to block the attack and saw the opening. When Duncan went for the counterattack, he was able to land his first blow of the match. Duncan swung again hoping to keep up his good fortune, unfortunately, Robert had hoped for this and again countered and laded several blows as Duncan regained himself. Robert tried both of these strategies throughout the rest of the match but Duncan now shy, only landed the odd counterattack and quickly went back into defensive stance. When Robert finally scored the last match point, it was one of the longest matches of the day. Duncan was disappointed that he was only able to land a few points.

However, Alex looked excited as he helped Duncan out of his armour. "What are you so happy about? That was a humiliating match," Duncan said, trying to wipe the smile off Alex's face.

"No, your first match was humiliating, but you've come a long way and this was a good result today. He obviously outmatched you, but you held your ground in defence, got the longest match duration of the day and managed to score a few points," Alex said, smiling from ear to ear and giving Duncan a pat on the back. "We have some time to spare now as you are one of the last riders in the final competition."

"Good, because I'm sore after that beating," Duncan said, holding his head where a large bruise would be in the morning.

Chapter 6

"**I** think we should start practice for the joust right away; there are three parts, and each round will end when a rider scores two or more points. The first rider to strike two unmatched blows wins the round. If the rider is dismounted, a bonus point goes to the other rider and the match advances to the next round. The dismounted rider stays off his horse for the rest of the event. We first start with tilting with a lance, then secondly blows with the battle axe, mace or flail, finally striking with the dagger or sword," Alex explained, as he passed the battered armour to his grandfather to fix up.

"That seems like an awful lot of things to cover," Duncan said, as he sat down with a pained expression on his face.

"Well, you already know the basics of sword play, and seem to be a quick study, so it won't take much improve your striking. You and Lightning seem pretty good together so we just need to practice with the lance on a quintain. I think Grandfather was setting one up earlier," Alex said.

"A what?" replied Duncan, as if Alex was speaking a different language.

"A quintain, it is a dummy with a target shield on one arm and a striking end on the other arm. As you hit the shield, it swings the striking arm back at you. It's a great way to practice your aim with the lance and to brace for the hit from your opponent. I read all about it in my favourite book about knights," Alex replied, as he searched a pile of books behind him, "Ah yes here it is. You should read it one day. I could teach you if you wanted."

"Why do I need to read? Once you have taught me these last few things, I will know all there is about being a knight" Duncan said, dismissively.

Duncan practiced on the quintain, missing the first couple of passes. When he finally hit the target, he was not ready for the quick counter of the striking arm and was knocked off Lightning before he could even register that he had actually struck the target. It took him a couple more passes before he was able to hit the target and be braced for the counter strike. Things were looking up for the lance.

"Next, we need to decide what weapon you want to use for the melee section. You can choose battle axe, mace, or flail," said Alex, as he was helping sort Lightning for the night.

"I like the sound of a battle axe, but what's a flail?" asked Duncan curiously.

"A flail is a mace with a chain between the ball and handle," Alex replied, as he started to think more on the subject. "I think it might give you an advantage as it adds speed of attack to a relatively slow combat. You also have the opportunity to strike a blow even if your opponent tries blocking the strike with his shield. The chain can reach around and you still have the ball hit your target. It also leaves your other arm free for a shield. The battle axe is a two-handed weapon. The chain can disarm your opponent if wrapped around their weapon."

"Sold, flail it is! I'll start practice tomorrow with Lightning."

"I think you should give that horse a rest and practice on your own two feet. I don't think it will be much to adapt the attack for use on horseback. But chances are you might be dismounted in the first round, and you'll need to be quick on your feet against a mounted opponent."

Duncan spent the next few days practicing with the flail on the quintain. Alex showed Duncan several disarming moves he had found in the book. They all worked really well after they had studied the diagrams and practiced. In the morning, he would add one more balancing routine that Alex would pick out to start his day. At night, Duncan honed his counter attacks with the sword.

The day of the competition arrived. It had been another rainy night, but just enough to keep the dust down in the jousting arena. Alex had been doing some research on Duncan's opponent. His name was Bruce and he was well known for his brutal strength. Alex and Duncan went over their strategy at breakfast. Bruce was not a fast fighter, so Duncan needed a good stance to be able to brace for attacks by Bruce and to be ready to execute counterattacks. This strategy would help take advantage of Bruce's lack of speed and help improve Duncan's odds of success.

Alex helped Duncan suit up and made sure all the straps were tight. Duncan picked up the first lance, and started to look nervous. With a look of pride, Alex reassured him. Duncan rode out to his starting side. His first look at the arena gave him a sense of awe. The size of the crowd and stadium put all other challenges he had done in the Gauntlet to shame. This was by far the main attraction, and the crowds in the stands showed it in numbers and volume.

After the rider introductions, the lady of the day dropped her handkerchief and the match began. The two riders approached one another with an enthusiasm that got the crowd going. A loud crack was heard as Duncan and Bruce passed each other, Alex closed his eyes fearing the worst. As Alex opened them, he heard, "First point to Bruce."

Alex caught sight of Duncan, who was barely hanging on to the reigns of Lightning and looked shook up. Duncan rode back around to Alex, who had a quick look over and gave him the 'okay' to set up for the next run.

Forever Knight

Duncan was now shy, having felt the force behind the first blow. As he started for the second pass, his nerves got the better of him and he was wide, so both riders missed the mark. Alex gave him a look of confusion and yelled, "You can do this!"

At the third pass, Duncan renewed his focus and put his energy back into the match. As the two riders approached, Alex could not force himself to watch and turned his head at the last moment. Again, there was a loud crash and lance splinters were all around. Apprehensive of the worst, Alex did not look and waited for the announcement, "Draw, no point awarded." Both riders were hit but no one was dismounted, so no better than the miss of the last round but better than the first round.

Duncan rode back around to get a new lance from Alex; his whole body showed the adrenalin pumping through it now. "You need to calm down and focus, Duncan. Yes, you got in a good hit but so did he," Alex said reassuringly. Duncan grabbed the new lance and Alex was not sure if he heard him.

He set up for his fourth pass; Duncan looked a little too enthusiastic as he started down the stretch. As they approached, Bruce mad a last minute move and Duncan was too late in adjusting. Bruce struck Duncan square in the chest. The blow knocked him off his horse and left him winded on the ground. Alex, who had watched this time, was quick to react; he grabbed Duncan's flail and ran out to help him up. As he approached, the announcer said "Point to Bruce and bonus for dismount. End of round one. Round two blunt may begin."

Alex got to Duncan and he still looked dazed. He gave him the flail and shook him. "Focus, this is round two now. He has the advantage of still being on his horse. You need to be ready for his attack."

Duncan, taking his time getting to his feet, looked around and saw that Bruce was being handed a large mace. The sight of this brought him back into the moment. He readied himself for the attack run. Bruce came at Duncan with full force, but Duncan blocked his blow with his shield and he had seen his chance. With his arm extended for the attack, Bruce had left himself open. Duncan started to swing the flail on the approach, and as it struck Bruce's shield, Duncan released and struck the handle of the mace. The chain wrapped around the handle as intended and Duncan started to pull. What he didn't see was the ball had struck the arm of Bruce and stuck. As Duncan pulled to disarm Bruce, he actually dismounted him.

The crowed cheered as the announcer stated "Point for Duncan and Bonus for Dismount. The score is now three to two for Bruce. End of round two. Contestants prepare for round three – blade."

Alex's face lit up, and he was surprised at this turn of events. He quickly grabbed the sword for Duncan and ran out to exchange the flail for it. After he handed the sword over, he noticed that Bruce was using a large two handed sword. Alex quickly said, "Attack on his right side. He has to use the sword as his shield and his right arm might still be sore enough for you to take advantage of."

When the two met in the centre for the final round, Bruce came out swinging. His massive sword hit Duncan's shield but thanks to his practice routine, he was able to avoid being knocked over by the forceful blow and regained his balance. The attacks went back and forth, and Duncan continued to work on the right side of Bruce. Finally, he saw his opening when Bruce winced at one of Duncan's blows; Duncan quickly made a combination move and was able to land a strike on the body for a point.

After the announcement they began again. Duncan continued to focus on the right side of Bruce and the strikes went back and forth being blocked and countered.

Burt came up to Alex and asked, "How's he doing?"

"It's tied three all, if Duncan can get one more point, he will win the match. That would be a great upset, don't you think?" Alex said, without taking his eyes off the match.

"Well, I just checked the score for the Gauntlet, and even if he loses this match, he just needs to hang on for a few more minutes and he'll win the Gauntlet" Burt whispered to Alex.

Alex did a double take back to his grandfather and then back to Duncan and yelled, "Stall!"

Duncan was distracted by this change in strategy and in that brief moment, Bruce let go of the sword with his right hand and landed a blow with one arm on Duncan's leg.

As the announcer stated, "Four to three for Bruce," Duncan limped back to Alex with a look of puzzlement on his face

"What was that… I had him, and then you start yelling something about stalling?" Duncan asked, with a disappointed tone.

"Never mind that. If you can hold out for a few minutes longer, you'll have enough points from time to win the Gauntlet," Alex replied.

"But I could have won, his right arm is hurt," Duncan stated.

"Don't count on that anymore. Did you see the way he was able to swing that sword with one hand, I think he has been holding out; his left hand is just as dangerous as his right. You need to be strictly defensive and hold out for time," Alex said firmly.

As Duncan was heading back to the centre, they all noticed that Bruce had changed his large two handed sword for a shield on his right and a lighter sword in his left. Bruce began the attack with such fury and speed that a defensive posture was all Duncan could do. At this rate, he would not be able to last a few seconds more, let alone a few minutes.

Duncan let up a little on his defensive stance and made his decision. On the next attack by Bruce, Duncan countered and landed a clean hit.

Alex looked shocked. Duncan had scored, and the third round was over. The match had ended in a tie. "What happens now?" Alex asked his grandfather.

"I don't know," he replied. "It's been so long since I've seen a tie."

The announcer came on and said, "Ladies and gentlemen, at the end of round three we have a tie. Contestants will now remount and we will cycle the three weapons, first to score an unmatched point wins."

"Well, at least this gives us more time," Alex said.

"No, they stop the clock for the tie breaker; he will have to score the point if he has any chance of winning the Gauntlet." Burt was viably tense.

The announcer spoke up, "The weapon will be lance."

Both riders suited up back on to their horses. They rode towards each other, lances held high. The lances lowered, and as Duncan felt the blow from Bruce, he could also feel his lance strike its target.

"Draw point, next weapon, blunt," the announcer said.

"Now I wish I had practiced on horseback," Duncan said, as Alex handed him his flail.

The two riders set up, Duncan with his flail and Bruce with his mace. As they approached each other, Duncan started to swing his flail. Once in range, Bruce struck first with a clean hit. Duncan would now have to land his strike for a draw point and go another round. His long reach was able to strike Bruce from behind. As Duncan was slowing down to turn back, he could tell something had happened. The crowed went silent and then started to cheer, as Duncan turned round, he saw what had happened. There was a dent in the back of Bruce's helmet; he had knocked him out and he had fallen off his horse. It took a while for Duncan to comprehend that he would get the point for a dismount and had just won.

It was announced that Duncan had won the joust match, and with these points he would be named champion of the Gauntlet. These words were a shock to him… and to the crowd.

The crowd went crazy. This was the first and only upset in the Gauntlet, as no competitor had bested a professional in any match this season, and to top it off, it was to win the Gauntlet.

Forever Knight

The rest of the day was a celebration for the underdog hero. Duncan received more adoring attention than he thought possible. He had not seen Alex or Burt since the win and was wondering where they were. They should be joining in the celebration with him. No one he asked had seen the two since the end of the joust.

It was almost daybreak before Duncan had a chance to get away and look for Alex and Burt. He found the two of them packing their bags getting ready to leave. "What's going on? You two missed what should have been the biggest celebration of your lives," Duncan asked.

"I'm not feeling well, and don't feel up to celebrating. I think I need to go back to my home and rest," Burt said, as he held onto Alex's shoulder for support.

"I wanted to congratulate you but you should have seen my grandfather last night. He looked a lot worse than he does now," Alex said, trying to hold back his disappointment in missing the celebration.

"Well, I feel like this victory is as much yours as it is mine. Without your help, I would most likely have come in last. Where are you going? Do you need any help to get there?" Duncan asked.

"That won't be necessary; it's only a half day's walk south of town, just before the river crossing. You can come and visit with Alex, as I'm sure he would like that after I have rested," Burt said.

"Yes, do come and visit us sometime soon. What are you going to do?" Alex asked.

"Well, I think I'm going to try and make good on my local fame. I saw an inn at the town centre. I'll get a room there and see if my champion status can get me a job. If not, a few free drinks from the local admirers will help!"

The three parted company with Alex helping his grandfather keep steady as they walked south back to their home.

Chapter 7

A week passed and Burt was showing no signs of improvement. One morning Burt called Alex to his room. "You need to start to pack for a long trip we are going to take," Burt said softly, without making eye contact.

"But you're sick. You shouldn't leave your bed, let alone go on a long trip," Alex argued.

"That's exactly why we must go now. I am old and sick, and you need to be with family," Burt said.

"Family? You said my parents were dead; you're the only family I have or need." A long look at his grandfather's face told him that he would not with this battle.. His shoulders slumped, he left the room.

With no further argument, Alex began to pack. Regardless of this bad news, he would always do as his grandfather asked of him. As he was packing, he saw a bright glow coming from his grandfather's room. When he went to check on him, Burt opened the door, looking better than he had in a while. His normally scruffy, grey hair was slicked back, and he had his traveling robe on and his cloak in hand. He had his backpack ready and a walking staff in his right hand.

"You look much better, so we don't have to travel anywhere," Alex said, after the shock of seeing the quick change in his grandfather wore off.

"This is only temporary. It changes nothing. Come on, we're going into town to see a friend before we start our journey," Burt replied, as walked out the front door.

Alex had to run to catch up; his grandfather had not walked so fast in years. "Who are we meeting in town?" Alex asked.

"Duncan. We are going to see if he would like to join us on our journey," Burt said, as he picked up the pace.

They found Duncan still at the inn near town centre. He was at the bar telling tall tales of his deeds, with several young girls hanging on his every word. When Burt and Alex came up behind him, he did not notice them. They recognized the story of the Gauntlet challenge but not all the details seemed right. "He was seven feet tall and I took him down with one blow; it set the tone for all the competitions to come," Duncan told of his first hand-to-hand match.

"He was five feet if that, and you lost if I remember correctly," Burt interrupted, startling Duncan.

Duncan turned around with a scowl on his face that quickly disappeared when he saw who the comment had come from. With a smile on his face, he said, "Burt, Alex! I was going to come see you in a couple of days. This is great!"

"Unfortunately, we're not staying long. We've come to ask if you are still seeking employment," Burt asked, changing the tone of the conversation to a more serious note.

"I've had a couple of offers. I wanted to come and visit you before I started anything permanent," Duncan said, with a confused look on his face.

"I'll give you our entire homestead and all our possessions if you accompany us on our journey north." Burt lowered his voice and leaned towards Duncan. "Plus, there is a sizable deposit of riches on the premises."

"Are we not coming back?" Alex asked. Both Duncan and Burt ignored the question.

"How far north exactly?" Duncan asked.

"As far as you are willing to accompany us. It should only take a couple months. There is bound to be some danger so I figured a big guy like you should scare most of it off before they get any ideas," Burt said calmly.

"Months... Danger!" said both Duncan and Alex together.

"If you want a real adventure to brag about, this will be it. I don't want to travel with just the two of us... an old man and young boy. That would just invite trouble," Burt said, trying to close the deal.

"When do we leave?" Duncan asked, with a glint of excitement in his eye and a growing ego.

"Tomorrow, first thing. Pack your bags tonight and get a good sleep; we have a lot of walking to do," Burt said, as he took Alex's arm and went to go and get a room for the night.

Tomorrow came quickly for Duncan, but he was up early. He went down to the stables to find Burt and Alex waiting for him.

"I see you kept Lightning," Burt said, as he fed the horse a carrot.

"What is a knight without his steed," Duncan laughed, as he stroked Lightning's mane.

They loaded up Lightning with their supplies and the three began their walk on the main road north out of town. The road was well travelled and it would be over a week before they would start into the mountains and less travelled pass trails.

Every night around the campfire, Burt told tall tails of great kings of old, brave knights and their quests, monsters that lived in the dark forests and mountain caves, wizards that could command the elements. The tales were either scary or funny, and most were farfetched, but some were told with such detail that Alex and Duncan could not help but think Burt had been there.

They got to the end of the main road; it stopped at the edge of a cliff with a wide river at the bottom. The road forked in three directions. Two smaller roads led east and west along the river; a third started with a rope bridge across the canyon. On the other side of the river was an open meadow that led to the base of the mountains they would reach by the next day.

"We will cross the bridge today and make camp on the other side tonight," Burt announced as he took off his pack.

"But it's early afternoon, we can still make some good time today. Why are we stopping?" Alex asked.

"The rope bridge cannot hold a lot of weight, so we will need to cross one at a time, including Lightning. Alex, you will need to carry most of the supplies across as you are the smallest," Burt answered, as he unstrapped the saddle bags from Lightning.

Chapter 8

It took the better part of the afternoon for Alex to carry the supplies across the bridge, one bag at a time, and make the return trip. After all the supplies were across, Duncan crossed with a long rope in tow. While Alex was hauling the goods across, Burt and Duncan worked on a harness for Lightning, as they knew the bridge would most likely not be able to carry the full weight of the draft horse. The rope was secured to a rock on the other side and a large tree on this side, and when tightened would take most of his weight and allow Lightning to cross. When Duncan was safely across and the other end of the rope secure, he began to coax Lightning onto the bridge.

When Lightning was almost halfway over, they heard a loud crash to the east, and everyone looked up the road. A stage coach had been knocked over on its side.

Without thinking, Alex began to run up the road and shouted, "We have to go and help them!"

"Wait, you don't know what is up there!" Burt shouted back to no avail. He turned to Duncan who was about to run back over the bridge. "Stop! First get Lightning across and then come over. I don't think the bridge will hold any more weight."

When Burt turned back to look for Alex, he was almost at the carriage. Burt saw three huge shadows come out of the trees from the side of the road. Without hesitation, he grabbed his walking staff and ran up the road towards Alex.

Alex had stopped short of the carriage when he saw the three figures moving onto the road. Alex could see that the driver had been killed; most likely what had caused the crash. The door on the top opened and two people crawled out, a man and a woman, obviously shaken from the crash. As they looked around and saw the three approaching figures, the man drew his sword and ran at what Alex could now make out as three huge trolls. The trolls were slightly taller than the man and slender. They had dark skin and moved quickly in their tight-fitting clothes.

The man fought with ferocity, but his effort did not last long and he was thrown back against the carriage with such force that the carriage moved and was now precariously close to the edge of the canyon. The woman, obviously in shock, jumped down and grabbed the sword from the man now lying dead against the carriage. She made the same attempt, but even with all her anger had no more success. She received a single blow that left her mortally wounded on the ground. As the trolls passed her, they began to push the carriage over the edge. The woman, with her last breath, whispered, "Leave our daughter alone!"

With that last statement, Alex realized that someone else was in the carriage. Burt had caught up to him, and with the same realization, the two ran towards the trolls. Burt looked at Alex and said, "You save the girl. I'll handle the trolls."

Burt reached into his pocket and pulled out a white crystal. He placed it on top of his walking staff in a notch that looked like it was made for it. Once the crystal was affixed, he stopped and drove the staff into the ground. A bright flash of lightning shot from the crystal and struck all three trolls. They stopped pushing and immediately turned their attention to Burt.

With the trolls' attention now away from the carriage, Alex moved closer. The electrical strike had started a fire on the carriage, and it was quickly spreading. He climbed on top and looked inside. There was a girl in a fancy dress who was not moving. She was still alive but unconscious. He did not think he would be able to climb inside and carry her out before the fire spread. His first priority was to put the fire out to give him time to rescue the girl.

As he climbed down, he saw that two of the trolls lay dead in the road and Burt was chasing the third down. Alex tried to stop the fire by smothering it with his shirt and then with dirt, but all that did was start the carriage sliding down the hill towards the cliff edge. Alex grabbed a wheel and pulled with all his might, but that only slowed the inevitable slide towards the edge. He then screamed to his grandfather for help as he began to give up hope. Just as the back of the carriage slid over the edge, Duncan grabbed the wheel beside him. The two of them were able to hold the carriage from falling any further but the fire was spreading.

Burt was closing in on the final troll when he heard the scream from Alex. He turned and could see Alex and Duncan fighting a losing battle. Letting the troll go, he ran back to help his grandson. The fire had almost completely engulfed the back of the carriage and was spreading quickly. With another jab of his staff into the ground, the fire almost danced into a ball and then shot towards the staff and was absorbed into the crystal. With the fire out, Burt grabbed the wheel Alex was holding and asked if he thought he could climb up and try to carry the girl out.

It took some time before Alex emerged with the girl on his shoulder. He carried her up the slope towards the road. Burt and Duncan let the carriage go, and as they watched it fall, they could see the shadow of the troll on the other side of the canyon. It had climbed down and up the other side and was running towards the mountains. Duncan said, "We should go and chase it down."

"We will pick up its trail in the morning when we are all awake and rested," Burt said, nodding his head towards the girl in Alex's arms.

They crossed the bridge where Lightning was tied up and made camp on the other side of the canyon. No one spoke for most of the night, avoiding the questions they had about what had happened that day and what they all saw Burt do to the trolls and the carriage. The girl, who appeared to be a year or so older than Alex, but not by much, lay curled up asleep in the blankets provided by Duncan and did not move for most of the night. Alex's eyes kept wandering over to her. She was the prettiest girl he had ever seen. The only thing exposed was her long brown hair in a single braid. Her dress was singed from the fire and Burt had placed a set of Alex's traveling clothes next to her for when she woke the next morning.

Burt finally spoke up as they sat around the campfire. "I guess I owe you two an explanation."

Duncan sat staring at the fire and did not say anything. Alex looked up with a smile on his face and said, "I'd say! Are you a wizard? Was that magic you used? Can you show me how?"

"Slow down there, Alex," Burt said, with a slight chuckle. "Yes, no, and yes. I am part of the Wizards Guild. In our minds, what we do is not magic, but it may appear so to those who don't understand. And yes, in time, you will learn to use the same powers I used today."

"That's great! Why haven't you used your magic before? You could have taught me so much already," Alex said, with even greater enthusiasm.

"That's a longer story and I feel I owe it to tell you now. So if you could keep you questions to the end, I will try and tell it as best I can," Burt said.

"I am not your real grandfather."

Alex's eyebrows shot up and his mouth opened, but Burt motioned for him to wait.

"You were given to me by the Guardians to raise and educate to become a member of the Wizards Guild. I felt that the Guild was becoming detached from the world and the teachings were becoming self-involved and not to the benefit of mankind. I thought for the sake of your teaching, you needed to be raised with the understanding of the people you are trying to help. I was just about to begin your formal education, but as fate would have it, I am sick and will not be able to even start your training, so I am taking you back to the Guild so you can be trained and become a Wizard."

At this point, Alex looked like he was going to explode with questions so Burt finished with, "Yes, Alex? What do you want to ask? Just one question, though."

"Okay, just one. Why me, what makes me so special?" Alex said, restraining himself from asking another myriad of questions.

"That's a good question. Due to the society we live in—we like to call it the Second Dark Age—disease and plague are able to run rampant and uncontrolled. Many generations back, after the start of the Dark Age, the monsters in their effort to suppress human growth developed a plague that affects the very young. While this plague does not kill, it inevitably shortens the life span of the population. To become a wizard you need to spend years of study and practice, years that most people from this time and place do not have.

"Take my own age, for example. I may not look too different from the town elders, but it will surprise you to know that I am twice their age. Where they do not have the skills, knowledge, or facilities to maintain their health, they appear to age faster than those unaffected by the plague. I was like you once, chosen from another time and place, before the great plague. Uninfected in my youth, I have lived a long life. With this time, I have had the opportunity to be of service to the Guild and to learn what is required of a wizard," Burt said, seeming to finish his story. He asked, "Does that make sense?"

"Yes and no. What do you mean the monsters are responsible for the plague as part of their plan to suppress humans?" Alex asked.

"That is one of the biggest masquerades, and it has been kept for centuries. The monsters were actually made by man before the uprising. They are not even monsters, but machine robots. You will not know of robots, but think of them as complex toys that can think for themselves. In the effort to improve the robots, we tried to make them think for themselves, while still trying to control them; they had commands not to harm humans.

"Over the years, they twisted the command to meet their greater objective of survival. They felt threatened by the events of the uprising, where our reaction to their independence made them fear us, and they saw us as a threat to their survival. By suppressing our access to technology and power, they felt they had removed that threat without harming us. This started the fall into the Second Dark Age, and to propagate the suppression further, the robots took the roles and appearance of monsters from our fantasy and literature. This allowed the robots to live on undisturbed and keep a frightened society by playing on our basic fears and folklore.

"The Guardians of Knowledge were formed near the end of the uprising. Seeing the course that was inevitable, they set out to try and preserve the knowledge that had been developed over millennia of human growth. They developed a crystal-based computer, a thinking box, to store and protect the works and discoveries of all mankind. The Guardians went deep underground. Their main goal is to protect this knowledge, to keep this knowledge in trust until one day when people are no longer suppressed by the monsters we have created.

"Their crystal was split three times; first into two pieces, then four, and then eight. These eight pieces were given to the Guardian Council to keep safe. As time went on and society fell into the Dark Age, the Council sat back and watched. Two members who could not sit back and do nothing started the Guild. They would find those in the world who were developing technology and take them into their fold. They broke small fragments of their crystals off and grew them. These new crystals did not have the depository of knowledge the originals had, but they had the potential to harness the knowledge of the user. They spent years perfecting their craft, and with the correct application of the crystal, the person's knowledge, and the power they tapped into from the earth, they could control the physical properties of the world around them.

"The original intent of the Guild was to steer humanity back towards progress and out of the Second Dark Age, but after many setback at the hands of monsters, I feel they have grown complacent again, with self-preservation as their only goal. That is why I felt it necessary for you to see the world before beginning your training, for you to understand what it is we are trying to fight for. So it is my duty to make sure you get to the Guild to be trained."

"So, with all your powers, you don't even need me around for protection, do you?" Duncan finally said.

"That's not true, Duncan. I am very sick, and I do not know how much time I have left. I need someone brave like you to protect Alex, just in case, and to see him safely delivered to the Guild. Sure I could handle most situations we come across with the use of magic, but that always draws a lot of attention and questions. We are less likely to be bothered with you travelling with us."

"This brings us to the matter of the troll. It is imperative that we track it down and destroy it. The troll saw me use magic, but it most likely does not understand what it saw, and that makes it all the more dangerous. It will head into the mountains and gather support and then come after us and try and destroy the power that I possess," Burt explained.

"But what danger is there, really, as you said they will not hurt us, Grandfather," Alex said.

"Yes, but that definition is open to interpretation. If we resist then they do not feel that they have hurt us; it is we who have hurt ourselves. If the secret of the Guild or Guardians is determined by the capture of my staff and crystal, then the secret that we have kept for so long will be targeted and hunted and will be lost, along with any hope mankind has for exiting out this Dark Age. We cannot risk the information we carry to be lost to the monsters of the world, and the best way we can do that is not to be hunted, but to be the hunter."

The next morning they set out towards the mountains, following the trail of the troll. As they approached the base, the trail veered to the west and Alex noticed a sigh on Burt's face.

"What is it? What's wrong, Grandfather?" Alex asked.

"I had planned on taking the mountain pass to the east, as it is much safer, but it looks like the troll is heading more west, deep into territory of many dangerous monsters. We need to pick up our pace and stay alert," he responded.

They came across a spot that had been disturbed. Burt stopped them and pointed out several marks. "It looks like it rested here in the clearing to recharge. There's a good line of sight for the sun. In the mountain pass, it will not have a chance to get this much of a charge again."

"What do you mean...charge?" Alex asked.

"Well, the monsters are not natural, so they do not eat food like you and I. They require energy and can get it from a variety of sources: heat from the earth deep underground, burning fuel, and even directly from the sun," Burt replied. "But we need to get a move on. I don't think it will be stopping to rest much more now that it has a charge and we have made up some ground."

Chapter 9

They spent the next three days going deep into the mountains. Over time, the girl regained her strength as she rode atop Lightning during the days of travel.

The girl had been quite weak and reserved, except when they had told her to put on Alex's clothes before they set out. She looked offended, which had surprised them. "I can't wear these," she had protested faintly. "These are boy's clothes. And anyway, they are probably not clean." She smoothed her singed dress, holding her head in a haughty pose.

The three of them looked at her. Duncan and Alex were confounded. She couldn't possibly travel in that fancy dress. And Alex was offended by her assumption that his extra clothes were not clean.

He was about to retort when Burt spoke up. "My dear, it will not be practical to travel in that dress. And it could even be dangerous to us all by calling attention to us."

The girl sniffed. She obviously could not argue with his logic. She picked up Alex's clothes and went behind some bushes to change. When she returned, she held out the dress to Burt. "I guess you should bury this so no one will find it."

Duncan took the dress from Burt and went off to find a spot. He held it reverently, almost, and looked embarrassed.

As Alex helped her onto Lightning, she felt a freedom of movement she had never known, and she told him so. Then she lapsed into silence, spent from her preparations, and said no more than a few words for the next couple of days. It was clear that she was grieving and exhausted.

When they stopped to make camp for the third night, she told them her name was Sarah. She did not talk much more, and they all gave her the space they thought she needed after what she had gone through and figured she would talk about it in time.

During the days, they followed narrow paths that led up steep slopes. And most of the time, they had trouble getting Lightning up the paths. The trail came to the base cliff wall and went into a cave opening. Burt took out a lantern from his pack and lit it with his staff. As they followed the trail into the mountain, the path went downwards deeper into the ground. The cave opened up to a cathedral room. The walls and ceiling were a light with a faint glow, and as they got closer, they could see that the chamber was filled with mountains of gold, jewels, and an abundance of weaponry.

"This must be a dragon's lair; they are notorious for raiding castle treasuries and vaults, to keep anyone from gaining too much wealth and power to raise an army against them. They usually stay near large sources of heat; there must be some geothermal source nearby," Burt explained, as he led the group along the path that split the mountains of wealth.

Sure enough, as they rounded one pile of gold, they could see that the edge of the cliff seemed to be radiating heat. The path took them closer and they could see down deep into the chasm a flow of lava, the glow of which was lighting the chamber, and the reflection from the piles of gold made the room dance with yellow light.

"Yes, most definitely a dragon's lair. Now, it is important that we do not disturb anything. We should pick up our pace and get out of here as quickly as possible," Burt said, as he led them along the path that now sloped upwards and out of the cave on the far side.

The path continued to climb for most of the day. As they neared the top of the pass, they could see a figure standing in the light as the sun was setting. "That's the troll; it must need energy after being in the dark for so many days. If I can reach it before the sun sets, I think I can end this," Burt announced, as he directed them to stay quiet and remain there.

Burt moved with agility that did not seem to match his elderly appearance, or the fact that he was terminally ill. He moved in the shadows up the path. When he was finally in striking distance, he emerged from behind the cover of a larger boulder and raised his staff to plant into the ground.

At that moment, a loud roar beckoned out from the mountain peaks above them. This thunderous noise startled everyone, including the troll who turned around and saw Burt ready to strike. With the element of surprise lost, the troll took off. Burt did not pursue, but was more concerned about the noise he had just heard. He quickly scanned the mountain tops and saw what he feared. He made his way back to the group. "Everyone stay still and don't make any sudden movements," he advised them.

"What is it, Grandfather?" Alex whispered.

"Over there on the peak to the left, you can see a shadow circling; it is a dragon, and it is moving our way… fast. Everyone stay still. Do not move. A dragon should not attack us if we do not pose a threat," Burt explained.

As the dragon got closer, the group began to realize the sheer size of the beast. The dragon's red scales glistened in the sun as it drew closer. It was heading right for them, and once it was close enough, it started to circle. This kept up and the dragon did not seem to be losing interest.

"This is not normal; it should have moved on by now. Did anyone take anything from the dragon's lair?" Burt asked.

With shame in her eyes, Sarah pulled a large emerald out of one of the packs on Lightning, and said, "I'm sorry; it was so beautiful. I did not know."

"You fool, you could have gotten us all killed over a silly gem," Burt said, scolding the girl.

Alex had been looking at how the emerald matched her eyes. He felt protective—and also guilty. He was also to blame. He stepped in front of her said, "It was not her fault; I took something, too." Then he reached into his pockets and pulled out two bags of gold coins.

"Well, we may still get out of this alive; quickly throw the gold and gemstone down the path to that clearing," Burt said, trying to remain calm.

The two threw the items as far as they could, just reaching the clearing below. Within seconds, the dragon landed in the clearing with a tremendous thump, shaking the ground. It scooped up the items in its front claws but its gaze remained fixed on the foursome above.

"But you can kill dragons like you killed those trolls, can't you?" Duncan asked.

"No wizard that I know of has ever lived to tell the tale…they are too big," Burt said. "He should have moved on already; I do not understand."

Duncan reached under his cloak and undid his belt. With a swift motion, he threw the belt over the edge towards the dragon. Attached to the belt was a glistening sword. The blade seemed to catch the light as it flew through the air. Before anyone could comprehend what was happening, the dragon leapt up and snatched the sword in his front claw. The breeze from the dragon's wings almost pushed the four over where they stood. As quick as it came at them, it was leaving.

"It seemed such a waste to see a sword of that quality just lying in a pile never to be used by a skilled hand again," Duncan said, trying to explain himself.

But Burt said nothing and motioned for everyone to press on; they had a troll to catch.

Forever Knight

Chapter 10

The group hurried over the pass and could see the troll at the bottom of the valley, entering a cave. As they approached the entrance, they heard a lot of noise coming from deep within. They left their packs and Lightning at the entrance, and Burt urged all of them to be quiet and move slowly. They started to see light coming from a larger room ahead. They kept to the shadows, and as their eyes began to focus on the room ahead, their jaws dropped in amazement and fear.

The entire room was filled with hundreds of trolls; all of them visibly angry and listening to one troll at the centre. After a second look, they could tell that the troll in the centre was the one they had been following and that he was talking about them.

"I have seen the power that this man uses. We have heard rumours of wizards with magic, but this power is too great to pass off as folklore. This is a threat to our existence. Whether it be called magic or technology, it is a power that we cannot let the humans have if we are to be safe. We can no longer stay hidden in the dark, relying on their fear and superstition to keep us safe. We must hunt down this man and all others like him, determine the source of his power, and eliminate it once and for all."

The trolls all yelled in unison and the one giving the speech seemed satisfied that action would be taken.

"There are too many of them; we need to get out of here before we are spotted," Burt said, as he turned the group around.

"But what about what that troll said, are they not just going to hunt us and the rest of the wizards?" Alex asked. But when he got no response, he looked behind him and did not see his grandfather. After searching around, he spotted him; Burt was standing at the opening to the main room.

Before Burt stepped into the light, he turned around and said, "Duncan, take Alex north and ask for the Guardians or the Guild. They will eventually find you, and if you could find a safe town for Sarah, I never meant for her to get caught up in this. Alex, I am sorry we have to part like this. I will always be with you. Now! Duncan, get them out of here!"

As Alex was about to take his first step to run towards his grandfather, he felt the strong arm of Duncan reach around his waist and pick him up. He was heading out of the cave away from the only family he had ever known and could do nothing about it.

Burt, stepping into the light at the opening to the main room, took his staff and placed it firmly into the ground, and said, "I think you are looking for me. Come and get me if you can!"

The trolls all turned in unison and looked the man in the entrance. Before they could move, with an arc of lightning emanating from the top of his staff, Burt had struck down the entire first row of trolls. The lightning had jumped from one troll to the next, turning the first row into dust. The now enraged group of trolls ran at Burt. Just out of reach, they were held back by an invisible force field. With another burst of electricity Burt continued to pick off the trolls at arm's length. With more and more trolls now joining the push, Burt was unable to hold them all back. He could not kill them fast enough and they were getting closer. Switching from lightning strikes, Burt reached up towards the ceiling, and as if with sheer force of will, started pulling on the rocks above him.

Alex, Duncan, and Sarah could only watch from the mouth of the cave. They could not see the details of the fight but the flashes of light and the noise from the angry army of trolls was terrifying. When Alex felt the ground beneath him shake, he realized that his grandfather was trying to bring the mountain down on top of the troll army. His last stand was to do what wizards over the last thousand years had not done, make a stand for humanity and exert a blow to the machines oppressing them. Once the weight of the mountain began to collapse the cave, a bright flash of light was followed by a blur exiting the cave.

"Grandfather?" Alex screamed, as he ran in the direction of the blur. He ran a few yards into the thick tree line across from the stream. It did not take him long to find the staff stuck into a tree like an arrow. Seeing this, he knew that this was his grandfather's last act, to sacrifice himself to keep the secret of the Guardians.

Duncan threw Sarah onto the back of Lightning and ran to get Alex. Alex tried to pull the staff from the tree but had to call Duncan to help get it out. Once they had the staff in hand, Duncan said, "We should not stay here. The mountain is still rumbling and there could be a chance of an avalanche."

The three set up camp for the night in the next valley. Duncan could see that Alex was grieving hard over the loss of his grandfather but did not know what to do. Sarah went and sat next to Alex and held his hand. Not a word was spoken the rest of the night.

In the morning, Duncan woke up to see Alex and Sarah still sitting next to the fire. He started to pack up and get ready to head out, saying, "Come on you two, we have a long way to go."

"And where exactly are you planning on going?" Alex raised an eyebrow.

"We need to take you north to the Guardians so you can be trained by the Wizards Guild, just as Burt wanted," Duncan said trying to calm Alex.

"The Guild has done nothing to help me or my grandfather; I do not plan on going on a futile journey only to be a passive observer of time. I plan to fight these machine monsters like my grandfather and revenge his death," Alex replied.

"Well, we at least have to take Sarah here to a nearby town where she can be safe," Duncan said, trying to change the conversation.

"Safe? My parents are dead, the man who saved me is dead. I will not rest until all monsters are dead, then I will be safe!" Sarah said, in a burst of emotion neither Alex nor Duncan had seen before.

"With this staff and the help of you two, we could do some serious damage to monsters. People deserve to live free from fear," Alex said, as he stood next to Sarah.

"But I promised your grandfather I would take you north; it is what he wanted," Duncan said, with diminishing enthusiasm.

"I was raised away from the Guild for a reason. The Guild has become stagnant in their fight against the machine monsters. My grandfather saw this, and I plan on making a difference. You were asked along to keep me safe. With you fighting by my side, I could not think of anything safer."

"I'll stay with you until you are ready to travel north, but you're crazy if you think I'm going to go looking for monsters to fight."

Chapter 11

Sarah and Alex spent the next several days talking about their newfound common interest. She fascinated Alex. She was a spirited and brave girl. They thought of various ways to lure, trap, and destroy monsters. During the times they were not scheming, Duncan showed Sarah combat moves and practice techniques he had learned from Alex during the Gauntlet.

Alex went off and tried to summon the power of the staff, concentrating and planting the staff repeatedly into the ground as he had seen his grandfather do. But the only things Alex seemed to create with any consistency were blisters on his hands.

Once they had agreed on the best plan to take down a troll, they began making weapons, and practicing combat techniques. The plan started off from what Alex could remember about a similar situation in one of the books he had read and what the characters had done to capture a large beast. When they had a working plan that they knew inside and out, they began the hunt for a target, looking for signs of activity in the same way that Burt had tracked the troll through the mountain. Even though they went over every aspect of the plan and felt they left no detail to chance, Alex felt he had let Sarah down by not making any progress on the staff and having no plan to use it to accomplish their goal. This was not due to a lack of trying, the blisters on Alex's hands had turned to calluses and most nights he had a headache from trying to concentrate too hard.

After longs days of searching for signs of something to hunt, they picked up a trail. While the signs were there that they were closing in on a monster, they were not the same signs as for the trolls. After several days of tracking, they caught their first glimpse of the beast they were tracking. It was an ogre. They tended to be larger and stronger than trolls and were more likely to travel alone. This one had pale skin and was bald with beady black eyes. It was much larger than the trolls they saw, both in height and overall size, and their sheer brute force was the biggest hazard, especially since they carried around huge clubs.

This was a good test of their skills. They surveyed the nearby area for a suitable place to implement their plan. Their plan had been honed and polished over the past several days. They needed to lure the ogre into a place that was a natural dead end. There could be only one way out. Alex would act as bait, drawing the ogre into the trap and when the ogre had followed him past the designated line, the exit would then be blocked off by lowering a gate. A series of logs hung from trees would swing and strike the monster, knocking it over and then the rope net would be dropped and secured over top of the ogre, holding it down. Secure and immobile, this would give all the time the two needed to destroy the monster once and for all.

Alex set up to draw the ogre into the trap. From a distance, he set his bow on the ogre and drew back for the first strike. The arrow flew true and struck the ogre in the back. Reaching around and pulling the arrow out, it seemed more annoyed than hurt. Turning around to find the source of the attack, it saw Alex as the second arrow struck it in the chest.

The ogre was now set on Alex, so it picked up a club and started the chase. With the initial separation gained by the bow, Alex had a good head start, but the ogre quickly closed the distance. As the ogre got closer, Alex needed to dodge flying rocks and tree branches dislodged by the swinging club behind him. Leading the ogre down the well-traced path toward the dead end, Alex ran through the gate and grabbed a rope against the rock wall on the far side. The ogre slowed when it saw that Alex was trapped.

Once the ogre had passed the gate, Sarah cut the counterweights and simultaneously lowered the gate, pulling Alex up high to safety. As the ogre tried to break out of its makeshift cage, it was hit with the first log. The ogre tried to block the heavy blows but Sarah and Alex worked together to coordinate the attack and hit blow after blow until the ogre was knocked over. They quickly released the ropes and started to tie the net down over the ogre.

As fast as they worked, the ogre continued to struggle. Before they could finish, the ogre managed to pull the stakes out of the ground and begin to break its way free. Sarah and Alex were trapped before they knew it. The ogre was free and had the two of them against the wall. Recalling what his grandfather had told him, Alex said, "Stay still, Sarah. They should attack only if we are moving."

They were trapped, unable to move, and the ogre was fixed on the two of them, seeing them as a threat, just waiting for them to attack again so it could defend itself and justify their deaths. The ogre could wait the two out until they starved; either way, they would not bother it again.

Without warning, the ogre was knocked aside. Duncan, in full armour atop Lightning, charged in and surprised the giant monster. With the ogre now focused on a new threat, Duncan yelled, "Go! Get yourselves out of here!"

Sarah and Alex ran out. Turning around, Alex saw Duncan fighting with the ogre. The ogre swung its club and struck Duncan's shield with such force, it knocked him off his horse. Lightning, startled by the strike, ran towards Alex and Sarah. Duncan, now on the ground, rolled to avoid the next strike from the club. As Duncan countered with a blow to the ogre's knee, sparks and green fluid flew from the wound. As Duncan tried to remove his sword, but found that it was stuck within the ogre's knee joint. Vulnerable, with his weapon ineffective, the ogre set up for a fatal blow. Seeing this, Alex reacted and planted the staff into the ground, screaming, "NO!"

An arc of electricity discharged from the crystal. The white light lit up the sky, as the bolts of energy spread out, hitting everything nearby. A powerful strike hit the ogre, knocking it back, but the rest of the electrical release hit nearby trees, starting a fire that was quickly growing.

Seizing the opportunity, Duncan got to his feet and pulled his sword from the ogre's knee and plunged it into the monster's chest. Seeing the fire grow around them, he turned and ran towards Alex and Sarah, who had already started to flee. With the extra weight of the armour, Duncan needed to mount up to keep up with the fast youngsters.

They travelled most of the night until they came to a river large enough to obstruct the path of the growing fire. The three, exhausted from their brush with death, sat on the river bank and watched the fire consume the forest on the other side of the rushing waters. The wind blew the smoke and fire away and up the mountainside, containing the fire to the relatively small patch of trees in the valley.

"Thank you for saving us, Duncan," Alex said.

"Well, we'd better have a more effective plan next time we attempt something like this," Duncan replied.

"Does that mean you're going to help kill more monsters?" Alex asked.

"Well, someone has to clean up your messes and keep you two out of trouble," Duncan replied.

"Do you really think it's dead?" Sarah asked, staring into the fire

"Well, if the young wizard didn't fry it, or my sword didn't stop it, the fire would have taken care of the rest, but I don't think we should rely on forest fires to do our dirty work. You need to learn to control that thing," Duncan said, as he tapped the staff in Alex's hand.

Forever Knight

Chapter 12

Alex worked with the staff but only managed to get the crystal on top to glow. He could feel the force of the crystal but was unable to use it.

The three re-strategized and looked for smaller monsters to sharpen their skills on. They sought out several goblins, as they were small and slow. They looked like a dwarfed version of trolls. After each attempt, their plan worked better than before. The plan was similar to their first attempt but now Duncan was the ground man, making their trap even deadlier. They were able to get a few goblins in groups up to three but had not tried an ogre since their debacle.

Alex continued to try and wield the staff, and through sheer perseverance, he learnt to move small objects with the staff, but nothing came near his burst of energy in the first battle or anything near what his grandfather did. He was still convinced that he could learn to use the staff and searched through some of his grandfather's belongings to see if it had an instruction manual.

Forever Knight

Alex found a small leather notebook of his grandfather's... his journal. He began to read it. He learned that Burt was quite the man of science and kept very detailed notes. One section talked about a liquid he had created once, along with its chemical components, physical properties, and the chemical reaction that took place when it burned. He began to read more intensely, feeling a connection to his grandfather that he had not felt in a long time.

They started tracking a lone orc. This was the largest target they had tried since the ogre. Orcs were generally slightly smaller than a full grown man and had a green piggish look to them. Each night, Alex continued reading the journal while Duncan and Sarah tended to the camp fire and Lightning.

One time, while Alex intensely read, his staff was tucked in his arm and resting on his shoulder, and it began to glow. Sarah was the first to notice this and she pointed it out to Duncan. The two of them gasped when a small flame arose on the top of the staff. Sarah yelled, "Fire! The staff is on fire."

Alex, distracted by this, looked up and saw nothing; the staff was not on fire and the flame had disappeared. Duncan and Sarah both assured him of what they saw. Alex thought back to what he was reading at the time and the pieces began to fall into place. He flipped through the journal and began reading. The other two looked confused but a few minutes later, the staff glowed and sparks jumped out of the crystal at the top.

Alex said, "Did you see it? I think I understand now. The staff allows me to harness my knowledge. But I need to understand how things work. Like at first, all I could do was move objects with it. That's because that's how I would do things normally. Well, that's my understanding. When I was reading before the fire, it was about the chemical reaction that takes place when liquid burns; the reaction that creates fire. Thinking about it made the staff produce fire. I've now found a section in the journal about lightning and, hopefully, sparks will come out of the staff.

"If I can learn about these things then I can use the staff to control them. I need to gain an understanding of things and how they work. Now I have the key to use this staff as a real weapon, I need to do all that I can to maximise its use and do some real damage. I need to find out more from this journal."

He studied his grandfather's journal, and found several key areas of knowledge: chemistry, biology, mechanical, electrical, hydraulics, and structural. But most of the topics that his grandfather wrote about were too advanced and Alex lacked the basic understanding of the subject matter to understand the complex notes. He needed to walk before he could run.

He was only able to practice control with basics skills like fire, telekinesis, and electricity. It was a slow process and they had many mishaps while practicing.

When they caught up to the orc, Alex thought this might be a good time to try to use the staff against a monster again. Everything went like clockwork. The orc was secure under the rope net and Alex approached with the staff, held it high and planted it into the ground. He tried an electrical shock. His aim was off at first, but after a few strikes, it only seemed to anger the orc. He then tried fire, which only managed to burn through the ropes. The orc tried to get up but Alex was using the power of the staff to hold it down. Seeing the situation, Duncan was quick to react and, with one swing of his blade, decapitated the orc.

After another almost failure, Alex decided he needed to learn more to be able to control and harness the true power of the crystal.

They had avoided towns up until now, sticking to the high hills where most of the monsters could be found. But things had now changed. Alex was on a quest for knowledge and the towns were the best place to start.

This would be a welcome change for the group, which was getting tired of eating rabbits and other game that Duncan caught. They planned to sell the pelts for coins to use in trade for the books seeking. They were all looking forward to sleeping on a bed in a room under a roof that did not leak; they had been moving about most nights, so they did not build a shelter and slept next to

Forever Knight

the fire. When it looked like it would rain, they built a lean-to, but it always had a few leaks when it rained.

Alex thought the best place to find knowledge was in books like the ones his grandfather had kept. The towns must have people with collections of books they had kept in their families. When they went from town to town, they discovered that books were hard to find. Most people could not read and therefore did not keep books. Worse, many books had been destroyed by monsters who wanted to eliminate any source of knowledge about technology, which was a threat to them.

Most of the old books they could get their hands on were novels, some were self help books, and not the scientific books that Alex was looking for. He taught Sarah to read the novels, but Duncan took no interest in learning.

Chapter 13

After visiting half a dozen towns with no further success, they met a man who told them of the town of Bramblestead, not far from there. He had heard of a book dealer doing business there. He seemed to describe him as if he were a black market dealer and not on the up and up, but he was able to get any type of book you wanted.

Seeing this as their first break, they set off to find the book dealer. They travelled three days' north. On the way, Alex found several helpful chapters in the self-help books they found in the towns they visited. They helped him concentrate, and he was able to improve his aim and the power of electrical bolts. On their last day, they could see the town of Bramblestead. It was larger than any of the previous towns, had fortifications surrounding the outer limits, and atop a hill in the centre of town was a small castle.

As they arrived, guards caught sight of them. There was a flurry of commotion and the guards closed the large wooden gates and took a defensive stance. The chief guard asked, "Where do you travel from?"

Forever Knight

Duncan listed off the last several towns they had just come from. The guards quickly raised their weapons in reply to this and said, "Be on your way! You are not welcome in Bramblestead."

"And what gives you the right to deny us entry into the city? What have we done that you are so afraid of?" Sarah challenged.

The chief guard replied, "We've just gotten word that Kings Crossing and Eastbrook, which you have just admitted to visit, have been attacked by a gang of monsters."

"What's that got to do with us?" Alex asked.

"As they were destroying the town and the villagers' homes, they said they were looking for three travellers: A knight with a large mount, a young wizard with a staff, and a princess," the guard said, as he pointed to them individually. "A description that fits the three of you."

"That's crazy. I'm not a wizard. I'm just a boy and this is my grandfather's walking stick. Duncan can barely pass as a knight, and Sarah isn't a princess. Look how she is dressed. Don't make me laugh," Alex retorted.

But Duncan grabbed Alex and pulled him away. "We need to get out of here. Something's not right."

Alarmed at this turn of events, they left and made camp in the woods. They talked about the situation, going over anything they had done that could have left a trail for the monsters to follow or why they would be searching for them.

Alex was confused as to why the monsters would attack a village, because from what his grandfather had told him, they would only harm humans in self-defence. These attacks on towns and villages seemed unprovoked, and the fact that they had just visited those towns made matters much worse. Those villages had no technology or gold that could pay for an army. They should not have been seen as a threat to the monsters.

Duncan reminded Alex that monsters will destroy buildings and kill anyone who attacks them. "What if these attacks are because of us? What if the monsters are really searching for us?" Duncan said.

"How could they know about us? We have been careful and not left any survivors in our attacks on the monsters," Alex answered.

They debated for a while longer but they all concluded that they needed to know more; it was too much of a coincidence and a risk to leave it alone. They agreed to double back and find out who this band of monsters really were looking for.

While travelling back towards Eastbrook, they passed several travellers who had all heard rumours of monsters near the mountains. It did not take them long to track the path the monsters were taking. It led deep into the forest to the foot of the mountains. That night, Duncan went off to do some scouting to see what they were up against. It was a group of four ogres. There seemed to be a leader different from the other three. It had a different look and walk about it. When the light from the full moon came out, Duncan saw what he could not put his finger on before – a limp in the leg when it walked; the scarred and burnt skin; and a scar on the chest where Duncan had plunged his sword. This was the ogre they had first attacked. It must have survived and been searching for the ones that attacked it.

Duncan went back to camp to tell Alex and Sarah. When he arrived, Alex and Sarah were both reading. He told them of the four ogres camped not far from them.

"Ogres? Four of them? I thought they were more solitary, and that it was trolls and orcs that travelled in groups," Alex said, with a puzzled look on his face.

"There's more." Duncan's tone was serious. "One of the ogres is the same one you two tried to kill when all this started."

"What! How can you be sure it's the same ogre? We all saw what happened. There's no way it could have survived," Sarah countered.

Forever Knight

"I know what I saw, and I think I know why there are four ogres. Just like the trolls who were forming an army to destroy your grandfather and his staff, this one sees us a threat and has enlisted the aid of other ogres to hunt us down," Duncan said. "We cannot afford to let these ogres continue to hunt us, hurting innocent people along the way. They must be stopped or they will draw more support from other monsters they come across and then we will have no choice."

"You're right, these people who helped us do not deserve the fate they received… all they did was help out three travellers. They fed us took us in and helped us find books for Alex, it is not fair." Sarah said.

"We have to make a stand," Duncan said.

"But how? We have apparently never killed an ogre; we barely made it out alive last time. Now we have to kill four of them?" Alex worried. As he paced back and forth

"With magic, or what passes as magic these days, your staff, we have the advantage," Duncan said, as if the answer was obvious.

"I'm not ready," Alex said.

"Well, you will have to be, or more people will die and this group will only get bigger and will eventually catch us. We can not run forever," Duncan replied. "You can do it, Alex. I have seen you practice. You have made considerable progress in the use of the staff. Plus, we know how to exploit their weakness; they cannot harm us if we don't move. We can split them up and keep them away from each other; they will just keep standing guard, allowing you to pick them off individually."

They spent the night discussing the plan. The rule, as they understood it, was that monsters could not harm people, and self-preservation was secondary. The flaw in this rule was the speed of the monsters; they could attack where you were going to be, so if you continued to move towards an attack, you were the one who harmed yourself, and thus, the monsters circumvented the restrictions.

The next day arrived and a light fog covered the forest ground. They were not sure if this would help or hinder their attack but now seemed as good a time as any to pull it off.

They approached the ogres from the south, with the mountain behind the ogres to the north. They started their attack on the group from afar. Sarah, with Duncan's bow, started sending arrow after arrow into the ogre camp. This distance would give them a head start and time to run away. When the ogres caught site of the three attackers, they set out immediately. As they were being chased, they split up. Sarah and Alex continued to run south and Duncan ran west to split up the pursuers. One ogre followed Duncan and three followed Sarah and Alex. Sarah continued to run south and Alex split off to the east, drawing the remaining three apart. Two followed Alex and one continued after Sarah.

Alex ran until the two ogres caught up. He stood still as the ogres circled and studied the staff in his hands. They would not harm him if he did not move, but they would take the staff, as they probably saw it as a threat to them. He waited until the two ogres were side by side and then made his move. Striking the staff into the ground to draw the required energy from the earth, a lightning strike jumped from the end of the staff and struck one ogre on the left, searing him. The ogre on the right was knocked back and singed, but quickly came to its feet and started to run at Alex.

Closing his eyes and fearing for the worst, he braced for the impact. Out of instinct, he put his hand in front of him as the ogre rapidly approached and heard a great thump. The ogre had run into a wall, an invisible wall that Alex had created. The ogre was dazed, and Alex was shocked and amazed at this unexpected result. He quickly replanted the staff in the ground and concentrated to make another lightning strike. This one struck his target and he was able to finish off the second ogre.

Alex ran back to find Sarah and Duncan. He came across Sarah first; she was standing in the middle of a clearing, trying to stay still. As Alex approached, he saw that the ogre was circling, waiting for Sarah to make a move, hitting its club on the ground next to her. The force of its blows was causing her hair to sway with the wind. She was pale with fear, and the ogre remained focused on her.

The ogre did not see Alex approach from the woods. When he was close enough, he planted the staff and hit the unsuspecting ogre. Seared from the electrical blast, but not destroyed, the ogre turned and ran towards the new target. It took another two blasts to take the beast down. Sarah ran towards Alex and embraced him, giving him a prolonged kiss, which took Alex by surprise and caused him to blush.

Not knowing what else to do, Alex said, "We have to find Duncan," and then took off running.

When they found Duncan, he was trapped by the scarred ogre they had first tried to kill. But the ogre was not solely focused on Duncan; he was keeping a watchful eye out. It had expected the return of Alex with the staff. As Alex approached, the ogre stayed behind Duncan, ,using him as a shield, as it had learned from their first encounter.

Alex tried circling around but could not get a clear shot. Duncan remained trapped between them and Alex could do nothing about it.

Assessing the situation, Duncan said, "Just do it. Take the shot!"

Alex was hesitant and replied, "No, I'll hit you, too."

"He must be stopped. You have to take this opportunity," Duncan replied.

"Not like this. There has to be another way," Alex said.

Alex continued to stare at the ogre in the standoff, and his eyes shifted to Duncan. They looked at each other and with a quick nod, they both reacted instantly. Duncan dove to the side and Alex stuck the staff into the ground, producing his lightning strike.

The ogre was prepared for this and dove out of the way of the erratic electrical strike. The strike almost hit Sarah as she approached the standoff.

The ogre gauged its position and made its move in the confusion. It saw Sarah standing off in the distance and ran towards her. The ogre picked her up and held her out. As Alex spun to set another strike, he saw that the ogre had taken Sarah, and he let loose a cry of anguish. The ogre ran into the forest and towards the mountains.

As Alex started running after the ogre, he shouted, "We have to follow it; we need to stop it at all costs. We need to get Sarah back."

Duncan said, "But we need to think about this. He knows about your lightning strike. We have only taken down those monsters not expecting our attack; the element of surprise has been our only weapon up until now. This ogre knows of your power and has adapted to this attack, made even more impractical while he uses Sarah as a shield. We need a better plan."

"If only we could get to the book dealer in town," Alex said.

"Perhaps we can," Duncan said, and he began to explain his plan.

Forever Knight

Chapter 14

The next day they finished their preparations, and Duncan set off to scout the area and track the ogre while Alex took Lightning and went back to Bramblestead.

When he reached the gate, he was stopped by the guards again. The main guard said, "Don't think because you three are not travelling together, we will let you in."

Alex dismounted Lightning then began to untie the bag secured to the saddle. He carried it over to the guards and set it on the ground. He motioned for the guards to look inside as he opened it. The guards looked inside, and then at each other. The guards said in unison, "Wait here."

One of the guards left in a hurry. A short while later he returned with another guard who seemed to be in charge. He looked into the bag and quickly closed it. Without a word, he grabbed Alex by the arm and escorted him into the city.

Forever Knight

"Wait! What are you doing? What about my horse?" Alex screamed, as he was dragged into the city.

He was led to the centre of town and up the hill. From this vantage point, he could see that this was the largest town he had ever visited. As he approached the gates of the building on top of the hill, its size became more apparent. It was a majestic castle in the centre of the town.

Alex was told to wait in a small chamber while one of the guards went through the main doors. A few moments later, he came back and picked up the bag, telling Alex to follow him. Alex followed the guard into the main chamber; it was the grandest room that Alex had ever seen. It had tall windows and a ceiling so high he could not make out details. The guard went up to the front of the room, where a portly man sat in an extravagant chair, not quite a throne, but close. When they were finished talking, the man said, "I am Duke Armond, and I am responsible for this town. Come forward, boy."

Alex walked closer and did not say a word, as he was a little unsure of how to handle himself in this situation.

Duke Armond broke the silence and started the conversation.. "I have been hearing tall tales from these guards. Why don't you tell me in your own words what has happened over the last several days that has my guards in such a frenzy."

Alex asked, "If I may?" as he pointed to the bag that the guard was carrying. With a nod from the duke, he grabbed the bag and went to the centre of the great room. He took the bag and dumped the contents onto the floor.

The room cried in unison with a gasp and then went silent. After a long time, Duke Armond said, "What's the meaning of this?"

Alex said, "I thought it best to show you rather than tell you. These are the heads of the ogres that we killed. I was travelling with two companions, and we escaped an ogre attack. On our travels, the ogres followed us; it was not until your guards turned us away that the ogres caught up to us. When they attacked, we had to defend ourselves."

One of the guards spoke up. "It is true. We turned them away last week, as we had heard that two towns had been attacked by four ogres looking for three travellers."

As part of their plan, Alex did not want to let the duke think that there was any threat remaining. So telling him about Sarah being held hostage and Duncan tracking the ogre might lead to more questions. For now, he wanted them to believe that there was no longer a threat and he was alone; otherwise, he might not let Alex stay in the city. Alex not wanting to lie thought misleading them was an acceptable compromise. His grandfather would not have approved if he were still around but he needed this to work for Sarah's sake. Alex tried his best to make his face look sad, "My two other companions did not return with me."

Duke Armond looked puzzled, and then spoke up. "I see only three heads; the guard said there were four ogres."

Alex replied, "After I killed the three ogres, the last one ran away."

Duke Armond laughed, "You? You killed three ogres! I find that hard to believe. I have sent many of my best knights to try and purge this land of monsters. No one has ever come back with any success, and most do not even return alive."

To which Alex replied, "Like I said, there were three of us," trying to mislead the duke that his companions died in the attack.

"So who were these travelling companions?" Duke Armond asked.

The guard replied, "Well, one was a huge knight, and the other a young girl said to be a princess. This boy was said to be a wizard."

"A wizard? Hmm, are you sure you're not just taking credit for the handy work the fallen knight you were travelling with did?" Duke Armond asked.

To make a show of it, Alex took his staff in one hand and made exaggerated gestures with his free hand. He was improvising, but with the basics he had practiced, he was going to combine his levitation of objects with a small electrical charge for effect. He focused on one of the ogre heads and began to lift it. The head spun at first then slowed as it rotated, looking around the room. For the finale, Alex applied a small electrical shock to the head. At first, the audience in the room was silent with awe, but the screams began quickly when the eyes started to glow and the ogre's head let out a loud growl. This startled Alex just as much, and he lost concentration, dropping the head and cutting off the unexpected power supply to the decapitated head.

Startled and having jumped to his feet, Duke Armond began to clap. "Bravo! Bravo, you truly are a powerful wizard and the last ogre would think twice about messing with you again."

Alex, trying to conceal his shock and look like the whole thing was planned, took a bow.

"A feast, in celebration of our little wizard and the beast that he has slain!" Duke Armond said. As quickly as the feast had been declared, servants were off to begin preparations. Alex was led off to a room where he would be the guest of honour for the night.

During the feast, Alex was swarmed by a throng of admirers all wanting to know the thrilling details of the battle to kill the ogres. Trying to avoid that topic of conversation, he subtly tried asking about books or if they had heard of a book dealer, but it seemed everyone he talked to either did not know how to read or had never even seen a book before.

Frustrated, he gave up for the night and went to his room to get some sleep and begin the search again when he was fresh and rested in the morning. Alex had just fallen asleep, when he felt a sharp jab in his side.

Chapter 15

"Wake up," he heard a man whispering. When Alex opened his eyes, he could see the silhouette of a man standing in the shadows.

"Who are you? What are you doing in my room?" Alex demanded.

"Shh, you'll wake the guards; I think you're looking for me," the man said.

"Are you the book dealer?" Alex leaned closer and whispered "Why are you worried about the guards?"

"Yes, I am the book dealer. My name is Thomas," he said, stepping forward into the light. "And if you don't know by now, then I'd better give you a quick history of our town. Owning books and, more seriously, selling books is outlawed. Strange things happen to people who read books; some people disappear mysteriously others are openly attacked by monsters. So many years ago, Duke Armond banned all books within the walls of the city. This was to keep the citizens of Bramblestead safe."

"Then why do you continue to sell books?" Alex interrupted.

"I am a business man, and the fact that what I sell is illegal means my profits are up and competition down," Thomas said, almost laughing. "So I hear you are looking for some books. How may I be of service?"

"I'm looking for particular books on basic science," Alex said.

"Ah yes! I think I have just the thing" Thomas said, as he looked into his backpack, pulling out a high school science book. "That will be ten gold pieces; you can pay, can't you?"

Alex, taken aback by the high price, had to think quickly, "Of course, but I do not travel with my gold for fear of pickpockets, bandits, and monsters. It will take a day or so to get you the money."

"Well, you seem to be famous enough, so I will let you have the book, and I will travel with you until I get paid," Thomas replied, as he handed the book to Alex.

"Do you have other books?" Alex asked.

"I do not carry all my books with me but I can get you just about any book you can think of," Thomas said, boasting.

"I don't know of any specific books I'm looking for but would be interested in browsing your supply," said Alex.

"Well, my books are far away. I can get any book you want...for a fee."

"That would be great. Plus, I need some time so I can collect my payment for you," Alex said, wondering if they even had ten gold pieces between the three of them.

They made plans to meet up outside of town the following day and start on their journey north.

The next day, Alex thanked Duke Armond for his hospitality, and now that vicious ogre attacks were no longer a threat, Duke Armond said that Alex was welcome back any time.

Alex left Bramblestead and was able to meet up with Duncan out side of town at their pre-arranged location before Thomas arrived. They discussed the situation and decided that if they wanted to rescue Sarah, they would find a way to pay the book dealer to get more books.

When Thomas arrived, he was startled to see Duncan. Thomas turned to Alex with a puzzled look "I thought your travelling companions did not survive the attack?"

"That's not exactly what I said but here's the situation. Sarah, the third member of our group, has been captured by the last ogre. I need to learn a new attack skill to catch the ogre off-guard and rescue Sarah before we can travel north for payment. Once she is safe then we want to find more books to help us on our mission. That's why I need to study this book and better prepare myself for the fight," Alex said, trying to get Thomas up to speed.

"Well, why didn't you just say so in the first place. I know all about that book, have read it many times. I can answer any questions you have. Plus, I have never seen an ogre before, let alone someone trying to kill it. As long as you don't expect me to fight, you can count me in," Thomas said, with a new enthusiasm.

Duncan laughed, looking at the scrawny book dealer. "I would not worry too much about fighting. We can hold our own without your help. We should be able to make it close to the ogre's hideout by night fall. We can get an assessment of the situation and make plans to rescue Sarah."

Alex rode on Lightning, trying to find something useful in the book while Duncan led the horse. Thomas walked close behind, answering any questions Alex had about sections of the book.

It was late evening when Duncan stopped and motioned to Thomas and Alex to remain quiet and dismount. They went the last hundred yards in short movements coordinated by Duncan. When they were all at the top of the hill, Duncan pointed out the cave where the ogre was keeping Sarah.

"He has been going out with Sarah in tow. She never leaves its side. I can't figure what he's doing on these trips, but they have been getting longer and longer," Duncan said.

"I think it has been trying to recruit. Look there, coming out of the cave, a second ogre," Alex said, as he pointed to a second shadow coming out of the cave.

"That's fantastic," Thomas said, surprised and overjoyed.

Duncan and Alex turned and gave Thomas a strange look.

"How is that fantastic? Now, we have twice as many to deal with," Alex replied in a questioning tone.

"You mean three times as many," Thomas said, pointing to a third shadow emerging from the cave, "and by fantastic, I only meant that I have never seen an ogre before; three together is almost unheard of."

"He was alone yesterday. We need to act quickly before it recruits more monsters to hunt for us. We need to head back to camp and come up with a plan for the morning," Duncan said, as he motioned for the other two to follow him.

Duncan had a small base camp set up not far away from the ogre's cave.

They did not make a fire so as not to draw any unwanted attention. They sat and talked by moonlight on the things that Alex had read and what he had a better understanding of.

Alex had made the biggest improvements in what he could do with his staff was an increased manipulation of objects. Before, he could make them levitate, now he could move them side to side and spin them. He got this from an increased understanding of momentum and forces needed to move objects. As Alex was practicing spinning a rock, out of curiosity, Duncan tried to grab the rock. With its ever-increasing spin rate, the rock sliced a gash in Duncan's hand. Startled, Alex lost concentration and the rock flew away from camp. Focusing on Duncan's hand and without thinking about it, Alex slowed the bleeding. Seeing this, he recalled the biology lesson he read and the basic first aid books he had browsed in the towns with doctors. Concentrating on the cut, he was able to close the cut as if it never happened.

"That's it. We can use that against the ogres," Duncan said, as he started to see a plan forming.

"I don't think you understand the concept of what we are trying to do here. We are trying to kill them not heal them!" Alex said back, in a joking tone.

"No, not that…the spinning thing. If you can do that to my sword then we can attack while it leaves its back exposed," Duncan said, putting the pieces together as he spoke.

"He will see me move the sword…it won't work," Alex replied.

"Not if I sneak it around behind it with the sword. He will see you coming and not expect anyone else. But, what about the other two, because I think that trick will only work once, as they seem to learn quickly," Duncan added.

"Well, that's simple. Just like we did before, try and split them up and use Lightning. As long as they don't have a hostage, they're vulnerable. I think I should work the rest of the night practicing wielding your sword," Alex added.

It rained hard all night and Thomas and Duncan barely got any sleep, but Alex was still hard at work with the sword. He was able to levitate the sword, move it up and down, slide it left and right, and spin it—and to top it off, he could make jabbing, slicing movements, at will.

Forever Knight

Chapter 16

After a quick breakfast, they set out to put their plan in motion. Thomas was to stay out of sight and follow whomever the ogre with Sarah was chasing. When the time was right, he would bring a sword into range and Alex would do the rest.

Alex and Duncan approached the front of the cave. After making enough noise to put a rowdy bar to shame, they got the attention of the three ogres inside. They emerged one by one and started to look around. Alex and Duncan stayed around just long enough for the ogres to catch sight of them and allow them to give chase. The scarred ogre led the chase with Sarah under its arm. Alex and Duncan took off in separate directions, and the last ogre started to follow Alex. Seeing this, the scarred ogre screamed and the lone ogre following Alex stopped and turned to reunite with the other two.

Seeing that they were going to reunite, Alex turned back and quickly pursued the lone ogre. Once he was within range, he struck the staff into the ground and started to build the electrical charge.

Before Alex could gain enough focus to execute his strike, Thomas came out from the bushes yelling, "Stop, Stop! You'll kill her if you strike now."

Surprised that Thomas would give up his position and the element of surprise, Alex yelled back, "What are you doing? I have a clean shot."

"Not with electricity. Look down at the water. The puddles are connected," Thomas shouted back.

Sure enough, as Alex looked down, the three ogres were all standing in a large puddle of water from the heavy rain the night before.

Assessing the situation and seeing their dilemma, the scarred ogre called the other two to join hands and keep contact with it. Once joined up, they slowly approached Alex, who was stunned as his plan of rescue had failed and his situation became one of dire consequences.

Duncan returned to Alex's side and said, "We'll get through this," as the two slowly backed up, preparing to defend themselves.

Out of nowhere, a flashing light came down on the arm of the ogre on the left. It was Thomas; he had struck with the sword unexpectedly from behind, cutting off the arm of the ogre on the end. "Now, Alex," Thomas screamed, as he was stuck by the free hand of the ogre in the middle.

Alex, looking down and, realizing that the ogres were no longer standing in the water, struck the staff firmly into the ground and shot a deadly bolt of electricity into the separated ogre.

Seeing his opportunity, Duncan took the lead from Thomas and severed the arm of the ogre that had struck Thomas down. Alex reacted quickly and, once the connection was gone, struck the second ogre down.

"Stop or the girl will die," the ogre bellowed.

At a stalemate, the three did not know what to do. The ogre rumbled, "Lay down your weapons. I will trade the life of your wizard for the girl."

"No, don't do it, Alex," Sarah screamed before the ogre squeezed her so she could not make a sound.

"The ogre is right Alex, you have to give up. We all do" Thomas said, as he put down his sword and walked around front with Alex and Duncan.

Duncan seeing what Thomas was doing, joined in and threw his sword away. Duncan said with slow words, "I guess our plan did not work, Alex. Now it's up to you."

Alex did not understand and stared back and forth between Duncan and Thomas, then finally back to Sarah. "I'm sorry, Sarah," Alex said, as he took his staff and lifted it above his head as if to throw it away. At the last moment, he planted the end of the staff into the ground. Seeing this, the ogre put Sarah out in front as a shield.

There was a moment of silence, and the ogre with Sarah looked up in confusion. The ogre looked shocked as a loud thud was made from something that struck its back. The first sword flew so hard into the back of the ogre, it pierced its chest and the tip of the blade cut into Sarah's shoulder. The ogre was still standing but dazed by the unexpected blow from behind. Turning to see who had snuck up and attacked it, it was only able to turn halfway around before the second blade, spinning in the air towards it cut its head clear off. The headless monster dropped Sarah and fell to its knees. Duncan ran in and picked up Sarah and carried her away.

"And if that did not finish you off, this should put an end to this," Alex said, as he concentrated and holding the staff firm against the earth, a direct lightning bold shot and hit the ogre's body, causing all the trees around to glow with the light from the bolt. Alex kept it on until the body burst into flames.

"Not again, enough with the forest fires," Duncan said.

"I think I got this one under control," Alex said, as he started to manipulate the fire and contain it on the remains of the ogre. "I practiced a bit with fire while you two were sleeping last night."

The fire burned hot and concentrated but did not spread past the burnt corpse.

Forever Knight

Once the fire was out, Alex walked over to Sarah. She was holding her shoulder as Duncan was trying to clean the wound. "Let me have a go at it," Alex said.

When the wound was clean, Alex put the staff into the ground and focused on the wound; slowly the blood flow slowed and it started to heal. He could not completely heal the wound, as it was much deeper than Duncan's cut on his hand. "That's all I can do for now, it should heal on its own."

"Thank you, thank you," Sarah said, as she threw her arms around Alex.

"Well, I didn't do that great of a job; it will most likely leave a scar. And plus, it was my fault the sword cut you in the first place," Alex said.

"No, you idiot. Thank you for coming back to get me, for saving me," Sarah said as she grabbed him and pulled him in to kiss him.

"Well, that may be an acceptable form of payment for some but I am still owed gold coins for my services," Thomas said, interrupting the two just as they started.

"And what services would those be," Sarah said sharply.

"Beg your pardon, madam. Let me introduce myself. I am Thomas, the book dealer. It is your friends who sought me out to help rescue you," Thomas said, while taking a quick bow.

"With the one book he sold me and his help, we were able to make the difference to save you," Alex said.

"And there are more books where that came from. Seeing what the young lad can do after reading one book, I think his efforts would be best served if I took you three to the great library," Thomas said.

"That's brilliant. Where is this great library, and why have we never heard of it?" Alex asked.

"Well, it's a lost ancient building that I happened across in my travels. It is the source of my business and I will show you the way for the cost of ten books."

Alex interrupted before anyone could ask the price of one book, "Well, the first one was a bargain so that sounds like a deal."

Duncan was slow to do the math but realized the situation… they did not have enough to pay for the one book they had let alone another ten. Remembering what he saw while scouting and tracking the ogre he spoke up, "What direction will you be travelling?"

"We have two weeks' travel to the north, why do you ask?"

"Well, I need to collect your payment. The ogre we just killed had a gold stash to the northwest, a day's ride. If you three head out, I can collect the payment and meet up with you along the trail in a few days' time," Duncan said.

"That'll work out fine. In two days, we should be going through that pass," Thomas said, pointing to a distant valley lined with mountains.

The four went back to their makeshift camp where Lightning was tied up. Duncan separated provisions for the three to carry from Lightning's saddle bags.

Chapter 17

While Duncan was away from the group, Alex approached him and asked, "What are you thinking; we don't have one hundred gold pieces. What's this nonsense about the ogre's treasure? Where are you going?"

"While tracking the ogre, I remember seeing a mountain chain to the north, just west of the valley you will be travelling. One of the mountains had smoke coming out of the top," Duncan said.

"A volcano! Are you crazy, you saw what happened last time," Alex said, in a whispered harsh tone.

"Not crazy, just lacking alternatives. If you can think of another way to get one hundred gold pieces then let me know. I don't particularly fancy the idea of facing another dragon," Duncan said, while sorting the provisions.

"Well, no I can't think of another way but perhaps we could make it safe. Last time the dragon noticed right away what we took, it must keep track of everything. We could trick the dragon; what if you took gold pieces from a chest, that would not be as obvious that anything is missing," Alex suggested.

"We could even replace the coins with stones of similar weight; a dragon may never even miss the replaced coins," Duncan added.

The next morning, the three set off by foot and Duncan astride Lightning took off. It was a day before Duncan made it to the base of the volcano; it was getting late so he made camp for the night. He woke early to search for an opening into the mountain, but searched most of the morning with no luck. Just as he was dismounting to have some lunch, he heard a loud roar. Startled, he turned to catch a glimpse of what he was expecting. The dragon sounded a lot closer than it was; it had just left from the cave entrance that was high up on the mountain, along a slim path that twisted upwards with sheer cliffs. Duncan quickly tied off Lightning and started up the mountain to take advantage of his good fortune.

Duncan spent the rest of the morning ascending the narrow path. With a constant feeling of nervousness that the dragon would return, he kept peering over his shoulder and scanning the sky for any sign of movement. When Duncan reached the cave entrance, the path was steeper and narrower. This time it was downhill, going deep into the mountain. At first, the light started to get dimmer; soon Duncan started to panic as he could not see his own hand in front of his face. Soon after, he started to second guess and saw the familiar glow coming from deeper inside the cave. It was the lava that the dragon draws heat from. As the glow intensified, so did the heat. Duncan started to worry that he would not be able to go much farther if the heat continued to rise, but fortunately just as this thought started, the piles of gold and treasure came into view.

It did not take Duncan long to find a chest full of gold pieces. He started to get greedy and was thinking of taking the entire contents of the chest, but started to worry about the sack that he brought even holding one hundred gold pieces they needed. There was also the fact that the dragon somehow knows when something goes missing. He managed to get the hundred pieces plus a few for daily expenses. He replaced the gold pieces with stones and covered them with the remaining gold in the chest.

Duncan made his way back to the outside and down the mountain to where he had tied Lightning up before the sun had set. He was constantly nervous and kept on the move, not sleeping, and with a close watch on the sky. It was two days of travel before Duncan finally had to grab some shuteye.

By this time, Duncan had made it to the pass where the others had gone. He figured he would be able to catch up to the group if he went hard for another day and night. Even though they were all on foot, they had made good time. It did not take long for Duncan to pick up their trail.

Duncan saw Alex first. They were breaking camp and getting ready to start the day's travel. Alex started to wave as Duncan approached; Sarah and Thomas came out to see what Alex was waving at. The three were delighted to see that it was Duncan. With Lightning back, they put most of their gear on horseback and that made their travel by foot a lot lighter than it had been. When they took their first break of the day, Alex pulled Duncan to the side.

"How did it go? Did you get the gold?" Alex asked in a whisper with an excitement he could barely hold back.

"I've got it here; it was just like we thought. There was a dragon and it left soon after I got to the mountain. Deep inside, I took the gold from a chest and replaced the missing pieces with rocks and covered them up. I haven't seen any sign of the dragon since I left three days ago. I think this will work. Here, you pay Thomas the next chance you get," Duncan said, as he handed the sack with the gold to Alex.

"That is a good idea; I don't want Sarah knowing too much about this as it makes me nervous as is. I will pull him aside after lunch and give him half now and half when we arrive," Alex replied.

Forever Knight

Chapter 18

Their journey north took them by several small towns but most nights they camped out under the stars. Thomas helped Alex understand more about the science and helped explain some of the items in his grandfather's journal. When they did pass a town, they traded for supplies and Thomas seemed to know who to ask about books. They traded for books using ones they had read for new ones to read along the way.

After heading straight north for most of their journey, Thomas directed them to veer to the east where there was no sign of a trail. It was more than an hour before the heavy brush let up and a path was visible.

The path led them into a valley thick with overgrown vines and trees. At first, they did not see anything until they were standing at a door. Once they knew there was a building in front of them, they started to make out the enormous size of it hidden under the vegetation and could not believe that just moments before they had not even known it was there. As they walked inside, the darkness was all-consuming. By the way their voices carried, they could tell it was a vast building.

Alex used his staff to light several lamps that Thomas had stored near the door. The little light that the lanterns gave off could not reach the end of the rows upon rows of books. This truly was a great library of past civilisation and it was hidden from the world... except one, Thomas.

"With the amount of knowledge in a fraction of these books, I could learn enough to destroy any monster. Not even a dragon would be safe from me when I have finished here. I will avenge my grandfather," Alex said, taking in the wonder of the library.

"Well, now that you have all these books, you won't need the rest of us, I suppose?" Duncan asked, suggestively.

"Are you kidding! We're a team, plus there are way too many books for me to research what is useful. I need your help to sort out the helpful books. Thomas, what about you, would you like to stay and help us?" Alex asked.

"As I have seen what you can do with a little reading, I would like to see what you can do after you read some of the more interesting books in here. I would be proud to be part of your team," Thomas replied, seeming to like the idea of having an eager pupil.

"So what about me?" Duncan added, "I cannot read, so how am I supposed to help?"

"I can teach you to read, just like I taught Sarah to read, if you are ready to learn. That way, you can help us find useful books," Alex replied.

"I would like that. Thank you," Duncan said, as he smiled.

"Nonsense, the two of you need to get your heads checked. I will teach Duncan to read, Sarah will start to look for books, and Alex, you will read and learn what you can. We cannot waste any time," Thomas said, as he grabbed Duncan by the arm and led him off.

"Well, I guess that settles it," Sarah said. "You go find a nice spot to read and I'll bring you some books that look like they might help. We have a lot of work ahead of us, so make sure to find a comfortable spot."

Alex found a quiet corner with some very large, comfortable chairs. By the time he had removed some of the debris and dusted off the chairs and tables, Sarah had dropped off half a dozen books.

At first they had a good system; Sarah would bring the books and Alex would meticulously skim the pages for useful information. He would ask her to find more advanced books in the areas he was interested in. Then, once Duncan and Thomas joined the books came a lot faster. Sarah would pre-read the books and mark the important and interesting pages, and Thomas would answer any questions that Alex had about the more difficult topics.

This went on for several weeks before Sarah started to notice that Alex was not going through the piles of books as fast as he once was. Soon after she noticed this, the piles of books grew faster and faster and she surmised that Alex had stopped looking at the books altogether.

When she found Alex to confront him, she was surprised to see a book in his hand. Upon closer inspection, the title had very little to do with their goal and looked more like an adventure novel.

"What do you think that you are doing," Sarah demanded.

"Reading, what does it look like?"

"You have not touched any of the books we have brought for you in the last couple of days. And here I find you reading a stupid novel," Sarah snapped.

"I am tired of study. I needed a break. I have been reading those mind-numbing books for weeks now, and I can't take it anymore," Alex admitted.

"Have you forgotten why we are doing this? My parents and your grandfather were killed by those monsters. The world is overrun with those beasts and I will not rest until they are all dead. The world is far too dangerous to be resting and reading novels."

A large crash, followed by the sudden sight of sunlight glowing off of the dust from the debris, interrupted her scolding. Alex and Sarah both turned to see a massive hole in the roof; they started to run towards where they had last seen Duncan and Thomas to see if they were all right and if they knew what had caused the roof to give in. They stopped in their tracks as the sound that echoed through the halls sent shivers up their spine. It was a roar that shook the floors and chilled their bones. It was unmistakable… they had both heard it before. It was a dragon, and quickly after the sound, they saw the massive head with glowing yellow eyes poke through the hole and climb down into the main room.

As Sarah and Alex stood there frozen like statues, Duncan came running down the isle.

Sarah was the first to speak, "Where's Thomas? We have to get out of here. That dragon is looking for something and we don't want to be in its way."

Alex and Duncan exchanged knowing looks and Alex said, "You're right. There's no time to waste, we have to get out of here."

"No, we have to find Thomas first," Sarah said, just before she took off running.

"You go after her. I'll look for Thomas down here," Duncan said, as he took off too.

When Alex caught up with Sarah, she was stopped, looking down over the balcony. Down below was the dragon, in the midst of a rage, breathing fire and knocking over rows of bookcases. In front of the dragon, and directly in its sight, was Thomas. Alex and Sarah were too far away from Thomas for him to hear their cries telling him to stay still.

Duncan came into sight on the ground floor at about half the distance Sarah and Alex were from Thomas.

Sarah yelled to Duncan, "Tell him to stay still, like Burt told us to do."

Alex added, "Duncan, the bag! Have Thomas throw his bag."

Duncan was able to close the distance slightly before the dragon saw him and cut his path off with a burst of fire. The building was spotted with fires and they were growing rapidly.

Duncan yelled at Thomas at the top of his lungs, "Stay still and throw the dragon your bag."

Not understanding and on the verge of panic, Thomas grabbed his bag tight and started to run for his life.

It was over just as fast as it began. A flash of fire hit Thomas square in the back, and the dragon took a quick leap forward and snatched the bag from the crisp grasp of the charred remains. The dragon was up and out of the hole in the roof.

As Alex turned to tell Sarah they needed to get out of here as the dragon was gone and the fire was the danger now, a beam from the ceiling fell and knocked the two over. When Alex came around, Duncan was helping him up.

"Where's Sarah?" Alex asked in a panic.

Duncan looked around and saw that she was pinned under the beam; it was too heavy for him to lift.

"Stand back, and get ready to grab her. I'll lift the beam," Alex said, as he planted the staff and began to concentrate.

As soon as the beam was clear, Duncan grabbed Sarah and the three were on their way out, the fire now raging. Alex had to stop several times to try and keep the flames from infringing on their escape

Once they were outside and clear of the building, Duncan set Sarah down. She was unconscious and had a deep gash along her side where the beam had hit. Her breathing was laboured from the smoke.

Alex wasted no time in recalling the first aid books and even some of the basic medical books he had read. The staff was planted and, one at a time, he concentrated and healed the cut on her side, pulled the smoke from her lungs, and addressed every bruise he could see. When he was finished, only her clothes showed that she had been in trauma.

She remained unconscious well into the night. When she woke, she asked for Alex. "Alex, the dragon, what happened?"

"It's all right, Sarah, we're safe now," Alex reassured her.

"The library, Thomas. Why did the dragon come now?" she asked in a panic.

"The library is gone. It burned in the fire. Thomas did not make it, and he had some of the dragon's gold... that's why it came," Alex said.

"Dragon's gold! You knew; you knew what was in his bag. Why did Thomas have dragon's gold?"

Duncan spoke up, trying to calm Sarah, "I went into a dragon's cave to get the gold so we could pay Thomas to bring us here."

"Both of you knew? You did this. You kept this from me and now you have killed Thomas and destroyed the library. You've ruined everything," Sarah said, as she started to sob and the tears flowed freely down her cheeks.

Duncan came and put a hand on Alex's shoulder, "Let her rest. She has been through a lot. We can discuss this tomorrow"

Alex was up most of the night, thinking about what to do, and listening to Sarah cry. It hurt him so much that his actions had caused this. In the morning, they all sat around and ate the breakfast Duncan had prepared.

Alex said, "I now know what we must do. I need to find the Guardians that my grandfather told me about. There is too much to learn, and with the destruction of the library, I know of no other place where I can learn. I have been a fool up until now, but no more. This quest is going to be my one true calling."

"That's great. We can be on our way today. We head north and they will eventually find us if I recall correctly," Duncan added enthusiastically. "What do you say, Sarah?"

"Take me home." Clearly, Sarah hade made up her mind.

"What? No! I am focused on our goal to avenge your parents and my grandfather. Why would you want to leave us?" Alex demanded.

"Because of your lies, a man is dead, and we barely escaped with our lives. I want no part in your quest. I wanted to kill monsters, not friends. Take me home," Sarah said, in a final tone that left no room for argument.

Not a word was said well into the night. Finally, Duncan broke the tension and silence by asking, "Do you know the way back to your home from here?"

"My village is called Knollside. I will know the direction once we get to a high point; it is to the west from here, at the base of Mount Titan. On a clear day, you should be able to see it even from this far away," she replied.

Chapter 19

The next morning, they packed up and went back to the main trail. They headed out west; it was several days before they had a clear enough day to see the mountain they were heading for. The trip was long, with little conversation. Sarah did not want to talk to Alex or Duncan, and Alex and Duncan did not talk much at all in fear of the disappointed looks that Sarah cast at them and the guilt they felt for creating that disappointment.

When they got closer to the base of the mountain, they saw a small gate nestled in the cliff that did not look like much. When they approached, the gate swung open without hesitation, and the guard behind the gate did not say a word as they passed. Alex and Duncan looked at each other, questioning this, but they both walked on.

As they walked into Knollside, Alex and Duncan were shocked by what they saw. The simple gate gave no hint of what was behind the cliff walls. The city was carved into the mountain. The stone work was detailed and colossal. The buildings went deep inside the mountain and the size of the city could not be judged by the building fronts alone. The two of them stopped and gawked at the wonder before them.

"Now that I am home, you two do not have to babysit me any longer. You can be on your way," Sarah said, without turning around to face them.

Duncan and Alex stared at Sarah, not knowing what to do. They both wanted to say something but did not have the words. They did not see any option other than to go on without her… this was the end.

Before either of them could respond or take a step, a crowd started to gather round, blocking all directions. At first, there were quiet whispers, growing into louder talk.

Duncan and Alex, not knowing what to make of the sudden mass of people surrounding them, moved to protect Sarah, standing on either side.

"Don't worry about me. They are friendly. You two can leave now," Sarah said in a curt tone, trying to hurry them off.

Just as Duncan moved to put his hand on Alex's shoulder with a gesture to leave, a piercing voice came from the crowd, "Princess! Princess, is it really you?"

Barging through at a fast pace was a short man dressed in expensive clothing. "Princess, it *is* you! You have made it back to us. We feared the worst when your parents' coach was found destroyed. We have been in mourning for your family, and thank goodness, you are back with us now."

"If that is what you command, Princess, then we will be on our way," Alex said facetiously.

Before Sarah could respond, the short man said, "Nonsense, you two are guests of the royal court; anyone who brings back our Princess Sarah should be given the royal treatment."

"And who exactly are you?" Duncan asked hesitantly.

"I guess the princess has not mentioned me. I am the court liaison. I handle all matters while the royal family is away and look after their every need while they are here. My name is Laurence," he said with an air of authority while straitening his fancy jacket and running his fingers through his short grey hair. "Guards, show these two gentlemen to our best guest quarters. Get them cleaned up and find clothes for them fit for the banquet we are going to hold in their honour."

With quick military precision, Alex and Duncan were led off before they could think of anything to say. The two enjoyed the treatment they got and were well rested and clean in fancy new clothing when escorted to the hall for the banquet.

The two were shown to empty seats on either side of Sarah at the head table. Alex could not believe his eyes when he saw Sarah. She was all done up in a fancy dress and elaborate hair. This did not look like someone who would be willing to travel on foot and camp under the stars, eating what they were able to catch that day. She was royalty, and he could not believe he had overlooked her regal bearing before.

When Alex sat down, he could not wait any longer. "So, you are a princess, and these are your people? Is there anything else that you would like to tell us?"

"I do not want to talk about it with you. Smile and eat your dinner. You can ask Laurence after dinner, as he likes to talk, and especially so after food and drink."

The three looked pleasant enough through dinner but did not say anything more to each other. After dinner, Alex and Duncan both approached Laurence, and as Sarah said, he was more than willing to tell the story of the city.

The family was travelling with a small amount of gold that was enough to get them attacked, as it was dangerous to travel with gold, but even more dangerous to have a large stockpile in one city. Now that her parents were dead, Sarah was leader of her people. He described how the city had to hide the fact that they have wealth. They travel across the region, distributing their wealth, and although they tried to avoid drawing attention, they attracted monsters looking for gold. They lent money to other cities with few stipulations, having them hold small portions of their wealth. The royal family was travelling to set up a new trade partner when they left. That was the last time anyone had seen Sarah.

The city was very prosperous; they mined gold in the mountains and tried to keep it hidden from the monsters by spreading their wealth across the land, but it had become increasingly hard to do so and they feared the monsters would follow the trail back to the village and attack and steal their wealth.

They had just learned that another gold transport had been hit last week; this time closer to the village than any previous time. It was attacked by a dragon; they saw the flames from miles away.

They feared it was only a matter of time before the dragon found the village and raided its stockpiles.

They feared to send any more transports out. The monsters were too close and would track the shipments back to the village.

But with the ever-increasing wealth stockpiling, the chance that it would draw a monster to the town was growing. That is why they had the shipments of gold sent out in the first place.

Laurence turned and looked at Duncan "Well, with another knight in our company, perhaps we could better defend against the monster attacks and even slay that dragon."

Duncan responded without thinking, "Well, I may not be the best knight in the land, but our little wizard here has killed his fare share of monsters in our travels."

Both Sarah and Alex looked at Duncan with surprise.

Laurence turned to the princess. "Is this true, Your Majesty?"

Sarah, not knowing how to respond, started to say, "Well, yes, but…"

Laurence stood up instantly. Cutting Sarah off, he boomed, "People, listen here. We have among us a wizard and a knight come to kill monsters and slay our dragon."

Before anyone could intervene, the cheers from the hall filled the air with excitement and joy.

Duncan and Alex were swarmed with villagers thanking them for coming to save their mountain village. This went on for most of the night and neither of the three had the chance to discuss what they had got themselves into. It was late into the night when the last of the guests had left the banquet hall and the three of them were alone.

Chapter 20

Sarah punched Duncan as hard as she could. "What were you thinking; now we have to answer for your careless thoughts!"

"I did not see you denying it when asked," Duncan responded. "We will just have to sneak out of town before this goes any further."

"We're not going to leave Sarah alone to answer for what we have all started," Alex interjected.

"No, I think Duncan is right. You two need to leave Knollside now before this gets worse. Surely, you are not considering trying to kill a dragon!"

"It wouldn't hurt to look into it. Perhaps there are alternatives we have not even considered. Killing a dragon is something my grandfather would not even dare, but he always told me there is more than one way to skin a cat, and we will never know if we do not try." Alex ended the conversation and not a further word was said that night.

In the morning, Sarah and Duncan came down to breakfast to find Alex and Laurence already talking.

"Dragons usually stay in volcanoes; do you know where the dragon came from and if there are any volcanoes in that direction?" Alex asked

"We did not see the dragon, but this mountain range is well known to us as we have all travelled it from a young age. The caravan that was attacked travelled south from here. We did not see the dragon pass overhead, and there is only one volcano to the south," Laurence responded.

"Then that's where we will look for it. We will head out and scout the mountain. I will not lie to you: we have never killed a dragon, but we will look and see what our options are." Alex stood tall and confident.

The two boys set off that day with a fresh horse for Alex and Duncan atop Lightning.

With the directions from a couple of the guards, it took them only a little over a day to find the volcano. The two spent the next day circling the mountain range, getting to know the lay of the land. The second day, when they saw the dragon leave the cave opening, both Alex and Duncan looked at each other and quickly headed up to the entrance.

After a few moments inside, Alex turned to Duncan, "I think we can do this. I don't want to explain now; I am still working the details out. I'll tell you and Sarah when we get back."

Sarah welcomed them back, "I thought you guys might have changed your minds and taken off while you had the chance."

Duncan responded, "Out little wizard thinks he can pull this off!"

"That's crazy! Not even your grandfather would attack a dragon, so what makes you think you can?" Sarah replied.

"I am not attacking it, or even trying to kill it. I want to trap it," Alex said.

Alex noticed some things about the dragon and the surrounding area and began to explain his plan to the other two.

"They get their energy from the volcano's heat. The volcano we just visited was old and has a dwindling heat source, and it was not nearly as hot as the first one we visited.

"If we could draw the dragon out to attack another gold run, and keep it occupied long enough, I might be able to close off the heat supply. Then when the dragon returns, I think we might be able to trap the dragon in the cave. With the heat supply cut off and the cave entrance collapsed, the dragon would not be able to recharge, and it would never escape.

"We must send out as many caravans of gold as possible. This will help drain the dragons' energy and keep it busy. If we can spread the convoys out, it will have to travel father and if we are lucky it will have drained most of its energy when it returns. This will also give me more time to set up the trap at its cave."

"How do you plan to seal off the heat source?" Duncan asked.

"There was a lake higher up the mountain; I will funnel it into the cave by cracking the overhead rocks." Alex said.

"What makes you think you can do that?" Sarah added.

"I read one of the geology books, and as I remember it, the area is prone to earthquakes. It will take a bit of practice with the staff, but I should be able to release the earthquake energy and direct it to make a crack in the lake bed. The water should drain into the cave and cool the top layer of lava, sealing off the magma and heat source below. When the dragon returns, if we can collapse the cave entrance, we can trap it inside. The dragon should be too drained from the raiding the caravans and not have enough energy to break through to recharge or escape. It will be sealed off, not able to look for another source of energy, and trapped forever—problem solved."

Alex tried to remember the main points from the geology book. He also worked with the head stone mason to fill in some of the gaps and get rock-splitting techniques. With this information, he used his staff to practice splitting rocks and shaking the ground.

Forever Knight

During the several weeks Alex took to feel prepared, the others started to prepare the gold transports and refine their part of the plan. They would have soldiers with each transport and make the dragon work for each one. They would also stagger the shipments and try and lead the dragon far away.

When everyone was ready, Duncan went out with the first transport to the spot where the last dragon attack happened. The other convoys went out in incremental distances away from both the city and the dragon's cave. Duncan waited until the agreed time when Alex should have been in position.

Duncan had been waiting for most of the morning with no sign of the dragon. He started to think that this part of the plan was not well thought out; they just expected to be attacked like the last gold transport. Out of frustration, Duncan kicked the chest of gold. The kick knocked the chest over and it fell off of the wagon. The subsequent crash and the noise of the coins spilling across the ground startled the men accompanying the wagon.

After the coins settled on the ground, Duncan heard a load roar in the distance. He pushed another chest over and shortly after, he could see a faint shadow rise into the air in the direction of the volcano. He told the men to drop the last remaining chest off the wagon until the dragon was closer and then to take cover and stay out of its reach. They had orders not to provoke the dragon and not to get close enough to be in danger.

Duncan took off to the other caravans to tell them to drop the chests and draw the dragon further and further from the cave to give Alex more time.

As instructed, the guards did not move, fight, or run, and in all attacks, the dragon never once hit a single person. It just took the gold and started to head back. Then the next caravan would drop its chest and the dragon would turn to track it down, each time travelling further away from its sanctuary.

"I can feel the dragon coming," one of the guards said.

"No, look! It's in the air. You must be feeling Alex's earthquake," another replied, as they braced for the dragon's attack.

Chapter 21

Back at the cave, the ground shook as Alex tried to crack the rock under the mountain lake. After several moments of violent quakes, he managed to open a route for the water to flow into the cave. The water came pouring in from the cave ceiling faster than he thought possible, and Alex did not have time to get out. Steam filled the cave and soon billowed out of the entrance. Visibility was gone; all Alex could see was white fog from the water encasing the lava deep within the cave.

Alex got disoriented and was soon lost. He could not his find way out of the cave, and the more he tried, the deeper he went. After several hours of aimless wandering, he heard a noise. Turning to see what it was, he could see a faint light growing in the distance. It was the light from the entrance of the tunnel, made visible by the dragon's wake in the fog. Alex made note of the location and waited for the dragon to pass before making a run for it.

Forever Knight

Alex reached the mouth of the cave and turned to seal the entrance. Planting the staff, he pulled down several large boulders into the opening and began to crack the rock above them.

Soon after the first boulders fell into place, he could hear the muffled roar from the dragon and its thunderous footsteps as it ran towards the way out. As the dragon blasted fire at the large rock, the scorching blast just missed Alex as the flames were directed to either side of the boulder that shielded Alex in the centre of the opening. Alex pulled down more rocks and sealed the opening again.

The dragon continued to attack the wall of rocks, breathing more and more fire. The rocks started glow red and were about to melt. Alex used the staff to cool the rocks and continued to add more of the mountain as a barrier. The rocks cooled, sealed, and formed a solid barrier; the dragon was running out of energy.

The dragon started to throw itself against the opening, using brute force. The intensity of the blows started an avalanche of rocks and scree that had already been loosened from the earlier quakes. The mountain came falling down in a sheet over the entrance and towards Alex.

Meanwhile, Sarah had travelled out to the first convoy and met up with Duncan. Seeing the steam and the avalanche from afar, they knew that Alex had done something, but they feared he might not be able to escape in time and were worried for him.

"We need to go see if he's all right. Duncan, gather a rescue party and meet me at the cave entrance, or at least where is should be," Sarah said, as she took off towards Alex.

When Sarah arrived at the location where the mouth of the cave should be, she could hear the dragon's muffled roar and a thumping that slowly became fainter. There was no sign of Alex; the mountainside was covered in fresh debris from the slide.

Deep beneath the rocks, Alex stood, absorbed in thought. He had to find a way to save himself. Mustering all his concentration, he used the staff to hold back the onslaught of rocks to form a protective bubble. For the moment, he was holding back the mountain of rock towering over him and threatening to engulf him. He prayed that he could muster enough power to keep holding them back, since there were just a few feet between the rock and where he stood. The staff glowed as it drew power to stave off the onslaught of the mountain. Alex fought to keep the rocks back, but they were so many of them, and the small rocks worked their way into his barrier. He was fighting a losing battle. As the rocks piled up to his shoulders, he lost consciousness from the lack of fresh air. The only light, which had come from the staff, went out.

On top of the rubble, Sarah noticed something different, something that had not been there before. She studied the rocks before her. Yes, there was a dent in a section of the debris that had not been there a moment before. And now she could see that the dent was growing. The rocks were sinking! She ran closer to the spot as the rescue party arrived.

After hours of digging, they managed to free Alex from the rock debris. He was covered with shallow cuts from the sharp rocks. He was almost not recognizable, bright red with burns from the steam and the dragon's fire. Sarah sank down next to him and laid her ear against his chest. In a moment, she cried, "I think he's stopped breathing!"

Duncan looked stricken. "It's tragic. "If only our positions were reversed, Alex could use his staff and first aid knowledge to fix all of this."

Sarah started digging at the spot where they had pulled Alex out. She quickly found the staff.

Running back to Alex, she thrust it into the ground and concentrated on anything she could remember to try and help Alex. Nothing happened, but she tried again and again.

Just as Sarah was about to give up, Duncan noticed something. He could not put his finger on it, but it seemed that some of Alex's scars were shrinking and the redness was slowly fading. Before Sarah could give up, he pointed this out and kept encouraging her. But nothing more happened that either of them could see.

Sarah collapsed with exhaustion and fell on top of Alex. She sobbed for the loss and her lack of ability to save him. As she embraced his body with hers, still holding the staff, it began to glow. Sarah could feel the energy from her body flow out of her and into Alex, and with a sudden gasp of air, Alex began to breathe. Sarah continued to cry and hug him.

As Alex came to, he said. "I'm alive. You can stop crying now!"

"These are tears of happiness, you fool," she said, not letting him go.

Chapter 22

Alex was only briefly able to attend the celebration back in town. It took several weeks of intensive healing and bed rest to get him on his feet again. During his recovery time, Sarah had taken on official royal business and Duncan had been making friends with the guards and a few of the knights. When Alex knew it was time for him to leave, he could see that his friends had found a good home. His heart ached, but Alex had decided it would be best if he went on his journey alone; he had burdened his friends with the danger of his quest long enough.

He packed up his gear, planning to slip out in the middle of the night to continue his quest to find the Guardians, to gain the knowledge to help fight monsters, and to avenge his grandfather's death.

When it was dark enough, Alex took a deep breath and quietly opened the door to his chamber. Before he had a chance to even step through his doorway, he was faced with the very disappointed Duncan and Sarah.

"You didn't think you could slip away unnoticed, did you?" Duncan's feet were firmly planted, blocking Alex's way.

"I was hoping we'd all stay around a bit longer," Sarah added.

Her words took Alex aback. "What do you mean 'we'?"

"What? Did you think you would go out and fight monsters all by yourself? You might just get yourself killed or worse, and then who would come to your rescue?" Duncan scoffed, with a slight smile.

"I thought you two were happy here. And Sarah, I did not think you wanted to travel with me anymore," Alex added, feeling cornered and taking a couple of steps back into the room.

"Nonsense. There is nowhere I'd rather be than with you. Now that Knollside is safe again, I will come with you and Duncan so we can find the Guardians and make the rest of the world safe, too."

"What about your people? They need you." Alex.

"Alex, my people are much better off with Laurence. If these last few weeks here have taught me anything it is that I do not know where to start, even for the day-to-day activities of ruling the people, much less the greater needs of the kingdom. I would much rather be on an adventure, seeing the world and helping you on your quest, than be trapped here as a bureaucrat." A faint blush had crept across Sarah's face.

Now, Alex saw that Sarah and Duncan had bags packed and were ready to leave with him. He grinned at them. With the three of them traveling together, there was no need to sneak out. "I assume that I can not change your minds?"

They both shook their heads, their growing smiles lighting up their faces.

"Well, then," Alex said, "we ought to wait till morning and say our proper goodbyes over breakfast."

The next morning they broke the news to Laurence over breakfast. He did not seem surprised. Sarah had not taken to the duties Laurence had given her and was constantly reminiscing about her past exploits. He had suspected that her decision was coming, so he only offered a polite protest, although he was sad to see her go.

There was not much time to prepare a send-off, but any plans they might have made would have proved unnecessary; the whole of Knollside turned out to say their goodbyes. It took most of the afternoon before Sarah, Duncan, and Alex had shaken the hand of every well-wisher and said farewell to their new friends.

The three set off, Duncan atop Lightning and Sarah and Alex on two new horses. They did not know exactly how to find the Guardians or what they would find along the way, but they knew they would be travelling the long road ahead together.

Forever Knight